Rich Rewards

RICH REWARDS

by Alice Adams

Alfred A. Knopf   New York   1980

THIS IS A BORZOI BOOK
PUBLISHED BY ALFRED A. KNOPF, INC.

The author would like to thank the John Simon Guggenheim Memorial Foundation for its generous help during the time that this book was being written.

Library of Congress Cataloging in Publication Data
Adams, Alice Boyd [date]
Rich rewards.   I. Title.
PZ4.A198Ri   [PS3551.D324]   813'.54   80-10214
ISBN 0-394-51101-8

Manufactured in the United States of America
First Edition

For my friends

Diane Johnson, John Murray,

and

Richard Poirier

Rich Rewards

Part One

1

More and more I have come to credit first impressions. People I have been crazy about on sight—Agatha, and in a different, much more violent way, Jean-Paul—I seem to love permanently. When I start with distrust or dislike, getting a whiff of right-wing politics, racism, arrogance, stinginess, to name a few unlovable qualities, I generally come back to that first view. I believe too that first events in a new place are significant, the way a city receives you, so to speak. If it rains, unseasonably cold, on your first week in London, you might as well push on to Paris. However, had I followed that rule and given up on San Francisco right away, I would never again have seen Jean-Paul.

My first week in San Francisco, then, was crazy and menacing enough to tell me that I might have done better to leave. Except that, like most people who come to that spoiled and lovely city, I had come partly for negative reasons: I was almost out of other places to go, and I was running away from a bad love affair in Boston. More positively, I was "doing" a house for Agatha (I am a decorator, of sorts), who had just mysteriously inherited all that money from the General, her father.

The arrangement with Agatha was that I should live in

her house, more or less camping out there, while I was doing it. In that way she would not be bothered with carpenters, carpet-layers, all those noisy people; I would cope with all that, rent-free, while she continued her diligent doctor's life —she is a pediatrician, specializing in infant lung problems— from the modest apartment on California Street, near Polk, where she had lived for years. Her new house was in Pacific Heights, one of the city's most expensive, conservative, peaceful, fog-ridden and beautiful neighborhoods—a curious choice for Agatha, the Episcopalian-radical, but she had fallen in love with the barny old house. I loved it too, although my stay there was strange and difficult from the start.

The first thing that happened, on my second day there, was that my garbage can was stolen. I had tidily taken garbage out the night before, leavings from my unpacking, and I had wondered why the can was so near the front porch, then remembered that there was no kitchen entrance: I would have to build a deck. And the next morning when I went out with more trash, there was no garbage can.

At first, I thought that it must be a San Francisco system of garbage collection with which I was unfamiliar, picking up the can along with the garbage. But this seemed impractical, and then I remembered the early Sixties, in New York, when people kept saying, "My God, they're stealing our garbage cans, what next?" Well, what came to be called "urban violence" was next. Anyway, there in San Francisco, my second day in town, my garbage can was stolen.

The next thing that happened, two days later, was the murder of a man, two blocks away from where I lived. Out walking his dog, one night, with his wife, and a car drove past, slowed up; someone stuck a gun out the window and fired two shots. A "random killing"—the dead man could have been anyone, or they could have hit his wife, or the dog.

I had gone out for dinner with Agatha that night, and so I didn't hear the shots, as I might have, or an ambulance, anything. I only read about it in the next day's morning paper, and although living in New York and spending time in Boston with my lover could have hardened me to murders, it had not; I was chilled, and terrified.

Going about my work that day, mainly walking slowly through large empty rooms and trying to envision something there—as I did that, I thought a lot about the wife of the murdered man. Married eighteen years, the paper said. If they had married in their twenties, she was probably about my age, around forty, maybe a little older. Had she liked her husband? Suppose it had been me, out for a walk with Derek, the Boston lover whom I had come West to escape? There was a sense in which I hated Derek, and not without cause, but would I have been relieved if he had been shot? Suppose that woman had really cared about her husband? And I wondered how she now felt about her dog, the innocent and unscathed cause of the walk.

And I wondered how long it would be before San Francisco more and more closely resembled New York. "Manhattanization" was a word I had already picked up from the papers, although I gathered that it referred to high-rise buildings, not to murder.

The third thing that happened was that Jean-Paul reentered my life—curiously, by way of the Sunday paper.

I was sitting at the table that I had set up in the middle of the kitchen, my island of order in what would increasingly be the chaos of remodeling, and I was doing several things at once: reading the paper (although I hated it, I was already addicted), drinking coffee and thinking about just where the deck should go, which window to enlarge into a door. The farthest southwest corner, I decided, the one that looked out to a tall clump of eucalyptus trees.

One advantage the Sunday paper has over the daily ones is that there are more of the good, nationally syndicated columnists; the daily papers tend to be incredibly *local*. I was reading such a columnist, a man whom I usually agree with and like, as he described a recent visit to France, and what he had gathered there concerning Euro-Communism, and Euro-Socialism. The most interesting, impressive man that he had spoken to, he said, was Jean-Paul ————, an economic theorist, professor, editor, who had said . . .

And so Jean-Paul, in that unlikely way, rushed back full-force into my life—or, rather, into my heart and blood—from across almost twenty years.

Where to start? I remembered everything about him all at once, an avalanche of vivid memories, under which I was suddenly buried: I saw our last parting, standing between trains, our eyes and our hands straining toward each other. I saw our crazy first night, the night we met, in the Club Méphisto. And I saw the beautiful unforgettable shape of his cock, and felt its taste.

To begin with that last, his sex: I had never seen an uncircumcised penis before, nor had that ever occurred to me as a place for kissing, for tongues. I know, unimaginative; but I was about twenty then, and the men I had made love with so far, including Marshall, my then husband, seemed not to go in for oral sex either, or perhaps not with nice girls like me. Anyway, Jean-Paul had a lovely cock, young and fresh and pink and delicately blue-veined, delicious.

Now, this is curious: all the greatest loves of my life, the four—or is it five?—have been uncircumcised. Even Jacob, who was Jewish: he explained that his liberated parents didn't believe in it—quite right, I think. What is strange is that this fact, foreskin or not, could not be known or even guessed at ahead of time, ahead of love. Also, there have been uncircumcised men whom I have not fallen in love with, just fucked—I mean, I don't automatically flip out at the sight of a foreskin. Just sometimes. I have wondered about my father: was he, as the French say, *entier?* No way to know; my mother would not have remembered, and anyway how could I have asked her? But actually I don't want to know about my father, whom after all I hardly knew, he died so young. I would prefer to believe that in some curiously effective way I was "imprinted" by Jean-Paul, phallus-wise, and such indeed would seem to be the case.

But I suppose I should tell about Jean-Paul in a logical way—causally, as it were.

In the middle Fifties I was living in London, in Kensington. With Marshall, to whom I had been married for less than a year, and with whom I was already not getting along. Marshall had money from home; he was studying at the London School, and I, doing nothing, was entirely dependent on him for money. In early November I persuaded him that a weekend in Paris would do us both good—and how right I was, although not in the way that I had imagined.

We found a cheap hotel on the Rue de Tournon. Marshall hated it—dusty, impractically shaped; I was crazy about it. In fact I loved everything in Paris on sight, especially those small, then quiet Left Bank streets, the gray façades of buildings, lovely scrolled balconies. If I believed in such things, I would think that I had lived there in another life, that I was recognizing my spiritual home; of course I don't believe that, but that is how it felt. I experienced a sort of euphoria, just walking around, crossing those beautiful stone bridges and stopping to stare down into the dark quiet river.

Small wonder that I should fall in love.

We had dinner in a cheap student restaurant, on Rue Benoit, and we responded predictably: I with enthusiasm, Marshall sourly. In fact our marriage was a typical Fifties error: I imagined that being married would rescue me from what had begun to seem a chronically turbulent sexual life—too many, too chaotic affairs—and Marshall thought a regular sexual life, in his case "intercourse" once a week, would free him for work. And in 1955, when we married, neither of those ideas would have sounded mad.

After dinner we went to a nightclub that someone in London had told us about—the Méphisto, on the Rue de Seine. And there was a tall, square-faced young man standing at the bar, with fresh fair skin and slightly slant blue eyes. A friendly smile. Jean-Paul.

He watched me as Marshall and I danced, he smiled as we sat down. He came over and asked if he could buy us a drink: had we yet tried Pernod? We hadn't, and he ordered some for us, a nice French host to visiting young Americans. He was about ten years older than we were, in his early thirties; an economist, he and some friends ("comrades") were just starting a magazine of political commentary. Most of this was for Marshall's benefit, I knew; he was waiting to ask me to dance, which he did, as soon as there was something slow, some oldy from the Forties. He maneuvered me out of Marshall's view, and we pressed together, barely moving. It was surely an instant, explosive attraction between us, but I was a little wary; I had had a few too many of those since marriage to Marshall—not acting on any of them, not yet, but still I was scared. Something must be wrong with me; I knew that marriage was not supposed to affect people in that way.

Surprisingly, I said that to Jean-Paul. "I'm really frightened," I whispered to his ear.

"Do not be. I can tell, you are a wonderful woman."

I imagined that to him "wonderful" just meant big, especially big-breasted; still, it was gratifying, even exciting to hear.

The evening went on more or less like that, sexy dancing alternating with intellectual discussion: the deposition of Stalin by Khrushchev, the revolt of Polish workers in Poznan. Jean-Paul approved of both, although he carefully explained that he was a Socialist, a non-Communist.

We all got very, very drunk. But I still do not quite understand how the next thing happened, which was—the three of us went back to our hotel, mine and Marshall's, and we all fell into bed together.

Oh yes, one would say in the Seventies, well, of course: threesies. But it wasn't like that, really. None of us was "into" kinky sex; we hadn't even heard of it, although the idea must have been somewhere in our minds. More explicitly, there was some token reason for the arrangement: the Métro had closed down for the night, and Jean-Paul lived out near the Place d'Italie, something like that. Anyway, there the three of us were, stripped down to a few modest undergarments, in our bed. Me in between the two men.

Drunkenness put Marshall instantly to sleep, and he was always an exceptionally heavy sleeper. I think that Jean-Paul and I were awake all night, wordlessly stroking, caressing— our hands making love to each other. Incredible, thinking of it now, to have been so drunk and so wide awake and so violently aroused, all night.

Around dawn I whispered to Jean-Paul that he should dress; I would meet him outside in five minutes. He whispered back that we would not have long; he had an important meeting at eight.

For the next couple of hours, we wandered around those streets, down to the river, beside it, in the chilly, rising mists, in the smells of a Paris dawn. I don't think breakfast, eating anything, occurred to either of us.

"You will come back? You could come alone, from London?" Jean-Paul asked me at some point.

"Yes, in a week or so I'll come." God knows how I thought I would manage this, but I knew that I would. I had to.

"I think that I love you very much," Jean-Paul said later, in a highly serious, considering way.

It was easier for me. "I love *you—*"

But how readily we both attached that word to all we felt, our whole complex of emotions, our lust and fatigue and simple human affection, simple curiosity about each other. In my case, love also had to do with prior loneliness, despair; for Jean-Paul it must have arrived confused with political idealism, hopes for mankind.

We separated on a corner near the Sorbonne, where Jean-Paul's meeting was, having exchanged addresses, phone numbers. Tears, and impassioned kisses.

I went back to our hotel and to Marshall, and that afternoon he and I took the boat train back to London. Le Havre, Dover, Victoria Station.

In London I began to go every afternoon to American Express to ask for letters, under my own, my maiden name, Daphne Matthiessen, that having been my arrangement with Jean-Paul. Every afternoon, as my heart pounded, nerves tightened, the clerk would leaf through all the letters under "M" and then, with porcelain English courtesy, he would inform me that there was nothing. After several days of this, I decided to ask also as Daphne White, using Marshall's name, although no one ever wrote us there. Jean-Paul had met me as

Daphne White; would he have forgotten Matthiessen, a harder name? No, there was nothing for Daphne White either.

Not hearing from Jean-Paul made me desperate, wild: I had to see him. Only much later in life did I learn that certain men, although they may love you a great deal, do not write letters.

For Marshall I concocted a story about a friend from my boarding-school days, St. Margaret's: Ellie Osborne was going to be in Paris for a weekend. She was terrifically rich, I could stay at her hotel with her, I wouldn't need much money. And she was such a rude arrogant person that Marshall would not like her at all. Besides, he had a lot of work to do, didn't he? And we had just been to Paris, and he hadn't liked it.

I did in fact have a rich arrogant friend from St. Margaret's named Ellie Osborne; Agatha and I used to imitate her nasal bray.

Marshall just said, "Okay, for heaven's sake, *go.*"

Next I went to a post office to put through a call to Jean-Paul, which took an hour of the most excruciating anxiety, ending with a terrible connection. Jean-Paul's voice faded in and out, as though drowning in the waves of the Channel which separated us. But I heard him say that he loved me, he had missed me horribly. He would meet me at the Gare du Nord.

It was a terrible trip, fraught with much more anxiety: I so feared that he had not actually heard me—one of us would get the time or the station wrong. What I really feared, but could not admit to myself, was that finally being together, finally making love, could not live up to the violence and weight of our expectations. In any case, on that Channel boat and then on the train to Paris, I was anything but a happy young woman, a budding adulteress, gaily off to meet her handsome French lover in Paris.

But he was there, beautiful Jean-Paul, as I got off the train; clinging together, we passed through all the barriers, we raced down long hollow corridors, we jolted along on the Métro, across the whole city to the Place d'Italie, where he lived. And we made love almost as soon as we were inside his room—one attic room, one big lumpy bed, chairs, books—and we were entirely delighted with each other.

How serious we were as lovers, though—how unrelievedly intense. It is amazing that we could stand it, with no leavening laughs, no simple silliness. We both behaved as though the world's future depended on the perfection of our congress, and very likely we thought that it did.

The room where we were, for most of that weekend, was large and bare, books being almost Jean-Paul's only personal possessions, and he could not afford many books. *Moby Dick, Ulysses, Don Quixote*—he seemed to have been fond of the heavier classics—and an enormous book that he later gave me by a writer of whom I had not heard: David Rousset, *Les Jours de notre morts*, about the concentration camps. I labored through it, a true labor of love, and of anguish; by then my pain for the lack of Jean-Paul was mingled with the horrors of the Holocaust.

But I now see that so far I have failed to give a sharply differentiated picture of Jean-Paul: handsome, virile, an intense young French intellectual—in Paris, in the middle Fifties. Surely that description would have fit a lot of young men at that time and place. Even the fact that he had fought in the Resistance, with the Maquis, and that he had a long scar on one leg and a minor limp—well, there were a lot of limping heroes around in those past days. But I supposed that he would remember me, if he did at all, just as vaguely: a big dark bosomy American girl, intense, with expensive American tastes—more about that humiliating last fact later.

I do remember what then seemed an exceptional quality of niceness in Jean-Paul; he was, and still is, a genuinely kind person. For example, this comes back: when I told him, what I had never said to a lover before, that such large breasts were quite a nuisance to me, so heavy and shapeless, really— instead of telling me that they were beautiful, terrific breasts, which I would have known to be untrue, in a very consider- ing way he said, "I used to have a girl friend, here in Paris, and her breasts were what they call perfect. But your breasts, they *say* something to me, they are yours."

Of course I loved him. Totally.

Between us that weekend we had almost no money. With a couple of implausible phone calls to Marshall, I had stretched the time out to almost a week: I was sick, I stupidly said. True to my begging description, my story about staying with rich Ellie Osborne, I had brought almost no money with me, and Jean-Paul was living on some sort of instructor's stipend. We subsisted on eggs and cheese, occasionally some grapes— that fall, especially beautiful: perfectly rounded, an ashy dark blue and wet and sweet. We drank a little wine.

We walked: up through steep Rue Mouffetard, with its tempting open markets, occasionally as far as Boulevard Saint-Michel, and down to the Seine, passing but not stopping at those student cafés, those terraces of unconsciously jab- bering people. Walking, clutching each other, talking—what about I cannot remember at all. I suppose we talked about our love and desperation, our hopelessness. Or maybe the future of Europe.

And then, one afternoon, although absolutely in love—

this is going to be a vividly embarrassing moment—I was suddenly seized with a longing for a "perfect" martini. It was a hot day, but still, at this point in my life, I cannot think of a more boring, trite and exhausted topic than that of the perfect martini. (Several local columnists still seem to find it absorbing, which says a lot about San Francisco, I think.) In my mind—Christ, how inappropriately!—there arose a vision of the Ritz Bar in Boston, that small, whitely decorated room that to me, the year before as a Wellesley girl, had seemed a pinnacle of elegance. I wished that Jean-Paul and I were there, each with a cold martini.

"Do you know what I'd like right now?" I asked Jean-Paul, making it idle. "A cold martini."

He smiled, fresh-skinned, clear-eyed, beautiful and kind. "Well, there is nothing so difficult in that. Let's go in here."

And he guided me onto a small terrace; we had wandered across the Seine, and were somewhere near Notre Dame. He ordered a martini, *bien froid*. And I got, of course, a glass of dark sweet vermouth with a twist of lemon and a piece of ice in it.

"It's good, but it's not exactly what I meant. It's different in America," I said, more or less explaining what must have been a clear look of disappointment.

It would probably be quite wrong to say that at that moment we both realized our futures did not lie together; quite possibly Jean-Paul, a realist, knew all along that I was just a big sexy American girl about whom he felt very intensely, for a while. Still, it is significant that that episode so clings to my mind.

And I do not remember any conversations about a possible future together; perhaps it only now occurs to me that this might have been? At that time Jean-Paul was telling me that he wanted badly to write a novel, but he was not sure he had the time. He was more concerned with the direction of his party, the National Liberation Front, which was an amalgamation of Resistance groups.

And I was concerned with Marshall, my lack of money —those dull and imponderable problems.

Well, we finished our drinks, my martini and Jean-Paul's beer; we walked back to Jean-Paul's room and we fell into the tangle of his bed, and made love, again and again. Our lovemaking forms a sort of continuum in my mind; it was what we always did. No single act was more, or less, memorable than another. Conversely, I do remember one particular act of love with Jacob, in a motel room near Ocean City, Maryland, one August afternoon: my first experience of sex with grass.

Then the next day Jean-Paul and I stood in the Gare du Nord: desperately serious, as only extremely young people can be—near tears, saying goodbye. Even our last time together had been cut short: a political emergency.

Once back in London, I got very sick, almost immediately: it was frightening; I was sicker than I had ever been before—or since. Sick with love is what I thought it was, and in a way I was right; for one thing, all those walks to American Express, where I hoped for some word from Jean-Paul, in the freezing London weather, cannot have helped. When I went out into the air, it was as though I had been scalped; any wind went through my head like knives. At last I yielded and stayed in bed for a while, and I began to get well enough to quarrel with Marshall—dully, hopelessly.

Finally I did hear from Jean-Paul, who said that he had been too miserable to write to me. Also he had been much of the time in Italy; his party was trying to effect a liaison with the Italian Action Party, another Resistance splinter group. His life would contain much travel now, he wrote; he would usually be not in Paris, but he could always be reached through his mother, in Fresnaye, a small town in Normandy, near the coast. And he gave me that address.

Well, anyone could tell what happened next: the impassioned letters that slowly diminished in their frequency, their intensity. Until, one day, although I still thought of myself as hopelessly, permanently in love with Jean-Paul— and I may even have been right, as I now see it—I was also, in another way, "in love" with someone else. Or with several people; this would have been soon after my divorce from Marshall—a festive, liberating time for me, all around. It could have been more or less the same for Jean-Paul.

Once, about ten years after we had seen each other, many years after we had not written, finally, any more—in a lonely mood, no doubt occasioned by the demise of another love affair—I did write to Jean-Paul. I cannot remember what I said, probably some wistful attempt to recall our gone young passion. He answered with wisdom and kindness, no wistfulness. He said, "I think you have the need at this moment for an actual presence, a person there with you. And that I cannot be for you. I live with a woman whom I think of as my wife. But please to write to me again. I do not want to lose you this time."

But I did not write.

I have even been back to Paris a couple of times, and never called or seriously thought of calling Jean-Paul. I did, though, think of him; I wondered if we could be passing each other on certain streets, not recognizing each other. Once— such a mistake—I mentioned this fantasy to the man I was there with, mean Derek, and he said that most likely Jean-Paul and I had in fact done just that; we had passed and not recognized each other. He assured me that by now Jean-

Paul would be middle-aged and fat, an anonymous French bourgeois. And so, in a way, until that morning in San Francisco, I must have accepted that version of Jean-Paul. Middle-aged. Fat, unrecognizable.

And suddenly, that day in San Francisco, everything changed: there he was in Paris, a leading Socialist economic theorist, and I did not know what to do. I could have written to him, except that I didn't know where, and I did not believe his mother could still be there in Normandy, alive.

As I thought of him then, I had the most terrible sense of loss, as though lacking Jean-Paul I had wasted my life. As though everyone else I had ever loved had been a poor substitute for him.

And I saw that the true reason for not writing him was that I knew I could not have borne it if he did not answer.

2

On the evening of the day when I read about Jean-Paul, and he in that way came back into my life, I was to have dinner with Agatha, in a new French restaurant; it was out in what is locally called "the avenues," meaning a non-smart, middle-class area somewhat south and west of Pacific Heights, in the direction of the ocean but stopping short.

We had said that we would meet there, and I, chronically early and uncertain of the geography involved, got there first, and was seated at a small table. I ordered a glass of wine.

It was the sort of restaurant that began to be fashionable in New York about five years ago. French country style was the intent, although I am not sure that the whitewashed walls, brass railings and checked tablecloths achieved just that. But it was pleasant enough, and restfully uncluttered.

Dimly aware of music, records playing somewhere, I looked about at the other people, all of whom appeared to be as transient as myself; and I wondered, Is everyone in San Francisco basically a tourist? Is it "home" for anyone?

And then I recognized the music, I knew the songs that were being played. Piaf, Charles Trenet, Jean Sablon. Those piercingly nostalgic songs of love and loneliness and despair. "*Vous, qui passez sans me voir . . .*" And I, a forty-year-old woman, might as well have been an adolescent in a drugstore —Rennebohm's, in Madison, Wisconsin—listening to Sinatra, insanely in love with someone. I was "in love," and in that same ludicrous way, with Jean-Paul, who was now a man of fifty or so, whom I had not seen for twenty years. And I could not turn off those feelings.

But then Agatha came in—in the middle of "L'Autre Côté de la rue"—and some sanity returned to me. Her small, slightly crooked smile, her small voice saying "I'm sorry I'm late" were both so reassuringly familiar to me, and so dear.

I wondered if later on I would tell her about Jean-Paul, and decided that probably I would.

Agatha does not look much like an heiress, despite all the General's unaccountable millions having passed on to her. She will never look like a rich person, and that was to be one of the conditions of my doing her house: she did not want the money that she spent to show.

To me, Agatha seemed to look, and in fact to dress, much as she did when we first met, at St. Margaret's, more than twenty-five years back. Though this might be simply a function of my having known her for so long, a failure on my part to register change: the sort of persistence of vision that is often observable among old friends. We think our friend is the skinny, brown-curled person of many years back; we fail to notice fat and gray.

However, Agatha really was still a small neat person with indefinitely light hair and sad blue eyes. An off-center smile, small nose. She was wearing a dark blue sweater, gray flannel skirt. Only her boots were new and expensive, wonderful boots; in a minor way Agatha is a shoe fetishist, maybe because dainty feet are among the few things that she likes about herself.

Abruptly—before I had meant to, really—I said to her, "The god-damnedest thing happened to me this morning."

And I told her about reading the paper, and then, in a very condensed, dried-out way, about Jean-Paul, our time in Paris, all those years ago.

Agatha is probably the best listener I have ever known. The quality of her silence, her lonely eyes and her just-amused mouth all draw one on. I have talked more to Agatha than to anyone, ever.

At times I have worried about how little she says; even, sometimes, it has seemed stingy of her, to give so little back. But that is surely unjust. For one thing, her profession is so specialized: how could she talk about anomalies in the lungs of newborn infants?

Actually I too have put in a fair amount of good-listener time, but that has generally been with lovers.

"And so, I don't know what to do," I finished, as I so often have, telling some story to Agatha. "Of course I don't have to do anything."

"You could write to Ellie."

Ellie was the girl whom Agatha and I had known at St. Margaret's, whose visit to Paris I had invented, my excuse to Marshall when I went back to see Jean-Paul. This has happened several times in my life, in fact: my lies come true. Rude rich unlikable Ellie had indeed gone to Paris, and she had stayed on there. It had never been clear what she was doing—very likely nothing at all.

Agatha said, "She might know something, just from reading the papers there. And writing her would be something for you to do."

Agatha understands me very well indeed, and what sounded like an idle suggestion turned out well.

Then Agatha said, "Next Sunday, some people have asked me to a party at Stinson Beach. Would you want to come? They said to bring a friend."

"Agatha, you know perfectly well they don't mean another woman."

"Oh, well, I'm tired of inviting men, especially when I really don't want to. And you are a friend." She laughed, in her sudden, private way.

I said okay, I'd go to Stinson Beach with her.

Dinner was good, we had fun, as we nearly always did; and we drank a lot of wine. We made our stupid private jokes, and heard more French songs. And by the end of the evening, although I could still feel myself to be "in love" with Jean-Paul, it seemed a more distant fact. Agatha often has that effect: she brings things into focus.

Agatha.

When I first saw her, in some bleak dormitory room at St. Margaret's, my first day there, I thought she must be someone's younger sister. But I asked her, "Are you a new girl too?"

"No, actually I'm the oldest girl around."

Actually. That word from that small pale girl, in her thin little voice, was funny and somehow appealing. I felt less shy, since she was shyer, less uneasy in that strange new atmosphere, a female dormitory—I was fresh from a big Midwestern high school.

"I've been here since kindergarten," Agatha told me. "I'm a fixture. I wonder if they'll ever let me graduate." She smiled, one side of her mouth going up more than the other. I liked her a lot.

We were both in our early teens then, Agatha and I, but while I could have passed for eighteen—and sometimes did, in bars, with older boys—Agatha looked about twelve. Maybe some awareness of how funny we looked together contributed to our becoming friends; in any case we were friends, right away.

St. Margaret's was, *actually*, a terrible school; without Agatha I would have had a very bad time there, and sometimes I did anyway. To begin with, I was sent there for somewhat punitive reasons: my "older" looks, my height and big breasts, especially breasts, were beginning to gain me a lot of attention at home in Madison; my nervous widowed mother was upset by those phone calls, by boys passing our house in cars and slowing up to honk. One of them had a horn that played "When my baby smiles at me"; my mother especially hated that. And she correctly guessed that I was wildly excited by all the attention. I was insane about boys; "boy-crazy" barely describes the degree of my mania. And the most depressing thing about St. Margaret's was that there were no boys at all, just letters from boys. With what violent palpitations I raced up the stairs each day to the pigeonholes of mail—very like those that I later suffered on the way to American Express in London, dying for word from Jean-Paul.

The other bad aspects of the school were pretty much standard: don't all such schools have bad food and ugly uniforms, and mean-spirited, unhappy teachers? And at St. Margaret's, a Virginia Episcopal school, what a ferociously snobbish lot those teachers were, impressed by Southern names, of which we had quite a few, and by Northern money—considerably less of that. They seemed somehow to have been misinformed about Ellie Osborne, however; she had more money than anyone, old New York money. It must have been her exceptional rudeness that led them astray; in their experience very rich people, rich Southerners, were also very polite, and so Ellie got none of the deference that she might have, and that certainly she felt to be her due.

Agatha's father was impressive to those ladies, being a real general, in the Pentagon; they always referred to Agatha as "General Patterson's daughter," which must have sounded odd when she first arrived at the school, a tiny six-year-old.

I did not impress them at all, in any way, with my flat Midwestern voice, my general inattentiveness and air of wishing to be anywhere else at all, which I passionately did wish. And I had neither a famous Southern name nor a mink coat to recommend me.

A word here about uniforms, and clothes: if, as was true at St. Margaret's, girls are allowed to wear their own clothes on weekends, the supposedly democratizing effect of uniforms is undercut, in fact demolished, so fierce becomes the competition over the Saturday night sweaters, the Sunday coats. I honestly believe that some of my later silliness about clothes, caring too much and spending too much money on them, may be partially explained by having had the "wrong" coat at St. Margaret's, wrong sweaters, no "good" pearls.

Agatha was not boy-crazy—nor clothes-crazy, for that matter. She did not correspond with any boys, and her only letters seemed to be from some maiden aunts in Richmond, and from her father, the General. But she could joke about our deprived sexual condition as though she shared my fervor, and perhaps, in an unformed secret way, she did. "Unmated in mating season," we lamented to each other in the springtime, laughing dementedly.

Agatha's mother had died when she was two, which is why she was sent off to boarding school so young, and I guess the condition of her having no mother, and I no father, constituted a sort of bond. We once worked up a fantasy in which our two single parents got married to each other, but even our active imaginations failed to bring that off: my reclusive, rather scholarly mother, and the playboy General? It would never work.

Certainly we were unlike in many ways, Agatha and I.

She studied hard and got top grades: already she was talking about being a doctor; at that time she meant to go to India and save everyone's life. I just wrote letters, all during study hall, and I drew pictures, cartoons of the teachers and the girls I most disliked, to make Agatha laugh.

I told her a little about my love affairs, and read bits of my letters to her, and she listened in that absorbed way she had, and still now has.

Once, the only time that I remember, the General came to St. Margaret's to visit his daughter. He had often promised visits that did not materialize; so deeply hurting to Agatha, I am sure, that she had stopped mentioning his promises. A rotten person all around, I thought. And on the occasion that he did actually arrive, he took Agatha and me out to lunch, and I found him a sorry disappointment; first, because he was out of uniform, in an ordinary business suit, and so being seen with him gave us no clout with the other girls. Secondly, he was a most unimpressive-looking man, small and pale. His hair was an unnatural shade of brown. Actually he and Agatha looked strongly alike, except that his face lacked the slight irregularity and thus the wit of hers. His manner was quiet, nondescript. Of that lunch I only remember giggling with Agatha and eating too much—boarding-school girls out for a treat. The General seemed distantly to disapprove; however, some vestigial sense of guilt over his less than successful role as a father must have kept him from overt scolding—and prevented him as well from ever coming back.

That day he gave off a sense of being in a hurry to be somewhere else. Later, when I heard more about him—from newspapers, *Time;* not from Agatha—it was hard to see that small mild man as the playboy escort of titled ladies. He never remarried, and was still swinging around Washington at the time of his death, a couple of years ago. And it was hard, too, to see him as one of the authors of our policy in

Southeast Asia. When I read about the banality of evil, General Patterson always comes to mind.

His money, of course, was, and is, the greatest mystery of all: how could he have amassed so many millions?

Since the school was Episcopalian, in a maudlin way we were all somewhat religious, weeping over Lenten hymns and full of Christian joy at Christmas. What I didn't know was how important all that was to Agatha; she really believed it. I was surprised, all those years later in San Francisco, to find out that she still went to church sometimes. "I'm a primitive Christian, with a very literal mind," she once explained.

After St. Margaret's I headed up to Wellesley, drawn by the proximity of all those men in neighboring schools, Harvard almost next door, and all those others within a few hours by fast car. Agatha went out to Berkeley, which seemed at the time an eccentric choice, and one which she did not explain: Agatha never explained anything. I now think she simply wanted to get as far away as possible from the General. She went from Berkeley to medical school at Stanford.

I married Marshall, went to England, fell in love with Jean-Paul, came back. I lived in New York and Washington, and went briefly home to Madison when my mother died.

By 1960, I was divorced, very broke and trying to be a decorator, a trade into which I had fallen accidentally: because I moved so often, people would admire an apartment, something I had done with it, pulled together, and they would ask, "How did you *do* that—get that?"

Most of my friends shared my own rather laggard and adversary relationship to the economy—professional people, "creative" people, who in one way or another were not making a lot of money. Who were enemies of the I.R.S., A. T. & T., the utilities companies. Small-time rebels, all of us. For such friends I would do apartments as cheaply as though their places had been my own; I liked to think that for them I could spend ten dollars and make it look like a hundred. But because of Wellesley, and other accidents of the time, I also knew a lot of rich people, and thus I got into a sort of Robin Hood situation: the money that I made from the rich helped me help my friends, as well as sustaining my own existence.

I was also embarked on a series of love affairs that were much more of an occupation than my work. And my love affairs were always expensive: clothes, my refrigerator stocked with delicacies, my bedroom with perfume and flowers. It frequently occurred to me that both my work and my life of love were seriously awry, but I could not see a way to change either one—or both.

While I was thus frivolously occupied, Agatha was getting through med school, then involving herself in the social protest movements of the Sixties. She marched on Birmingham, helped to register black voters, then lived and worked for a couple of years in Tallahassee as a free pediatrician. She got into the peace movement, and spent some time in the Santa Rita jail, having been arrested in Oakland at the depot from which napalm was being shipped out.

Meanwhile, back at his desk in Washington, the General was urging the bombers on: get Cambodia, back to the Stone Age with those yellow bastards.

But to talk about the General in that way is to denigrate Agatha's idealism, really. Hers was not at all a simple rebellion; of that I am absolutely certain. She believed entirely in what she did; in fact as she saw it she had no choice. When someone said that there was to be a demonstration at the Oakland depot, she had to be there, first in line.

By 1973, she and the General were not even formally in touch, and so it is strange that he did not rewrite his will, disinheriting her. My own idea is that, like so many people, he thought he would die if he made and signed a will; he planned to live forever. Stranger still is the fact that he turned out to have so much money. He had always lived in a high-handed, affluent way, Agatha said, but if she thought of it at all, she simply assumed that he must be very well paid for whatever he did at the Pentagon, and that he was spending all he made.

At his death, then, Agatha got over five million dollars, after taxes. And we talked endlessly, we speculated endlessly, about where he could have got all that money—both of us feeling, but not quite saying, that it must be somehow tainted. Blood money of some sort.

In any case, that is how Agatha, an unlikely person, came to be an heiress, and finally brought herself to buy a big house that she was crazy about.

And then she called me in New York.

She said, "You'll like the house. It's big, sort of crazy. Great long windows, and a yard with some old trees. I just don't know what to do with it."

I was thinking how surprised Derek would be when I left. Derek, my cruel lover. And thinking how, in a new and interesting place, I would probably not miss him at all. I might even give up having affairs altogether.

I told Agatha that I would get there as soon as I could, and I did, within a month.

3

There were many things to be said about my English Boston lover, Derek Churchill, and at one time or another I must have said them all: selfish, inconsiderate, self-absorbed, overweight and given to drink. But I said them silently, and only to myself. He was also bright and literate, sexually enthusiastic and, in his own dry way, a considerable wit. However, we were always antagonistic lovers, never anything like friends. Derek was not at all a "friendly" person, which could not be blamed entirely on his being English, although I tended to make that excuse for him.

He always looked and dressed like an upper-class Englishman, a banker or a publisher: sandy hair perfectly smooth; red-faced; in well-cut not-new tweeds. However, he was not what he looked to be, not a famous Churchill, but working-class, as he rather too frequently pointed out, calculatedly: he knew that I would like that fact about him, that I would not have liked it if he had been related to the Churchills. He was a lawyer, corporation law. An American convert.

We met, then, at a party in New York. He took me out to dinner, I took him home to bed—which could describe the beginning of most of my affairs at that time; I'm the wrong

generation for singles bars, and too shy besides. In bed Derek
was a great surprise; or I must have had some idea that Eng-
lishmen were always unremarkable in that way. He liked
me too; he thought our screwing was terrific. "My girl,
you're quite amazing" is what he said.
What is it that is so seductive about being praised in an
English accent? Maybe because the clipped sounds don't go
with the words? It is basically not an accent for enthusiasm?

Derek came back to New York the next weekend, and
a couple of weekends after that he invited me up to Boston
to see him, in his comfortable shabby flat on Chestnut Street.

We began to spend most of our weekends together, but
not all, and we never saw each other for longer than a weekend, except on that fatal trip to Paris—six whole days of
being together.

Since we spent much less than all our time together, it
was assumed between us without any explicit statement that
we both saw other people sometimes. "Saw" in that context
meaning fell into bed with, fucked. With me that was not the
case. I went out for an occasional dinner with an old friend,
usually a woman or some nice gay man. Never to bed. In a
sexual way I was completely addicted to Derek.

He did see other people, and what was cruel and un-
forgivable was that he let me know all about it, in his cryptic,
half-drunken English way.

For example, about six months after our relationship
began, I became aware that he was "seeing" a Radcliffe girl.
During one of my Boston weekends, it struck me that we
were spending an unusual amount of time driving around
Harvard Square, going to mediocre restaurants in Cambridge:
those were the earliest signs. Then he asked me why I had
gone to Wellesley; why not Radcliffe? Later he remarked
that he hadn't known until recently that Californians had

accents. "Curious, rather unlike other American speech." And so there she was: a Radcliffe girl, from California.

One night in bed he asked me if I had ever minded having such large breasts. I did not say, as I wanted to, You dumb jerk, of course I've minded. But I thought, Oh, hers are small, and no doubt perfect.

He had given me a whole girl, with whom I could torture myself.

At another time it became clear that he was seeing someone Spanish.

Of course, if I had confronted him with any of this, he could have thought and said that I was crazy. Delusional.

His delusion, a real one, was that I wanted to get married. Any slight complaint of mine, any hint that our getting along was less than perfectly satisfactory to me, and he would sigh, "Ah, well, my dear, I'm afraid what you really need is a proper husband, and you know that's not my niche."

I wonder if much younger women have this problem too, that of convincing men that they don't want to get married. I really hope not.

And although I genuinely did not want to get married—I had not liked marriage to Marshall at all, and I had never wanted to have children—it did occur to me that my clinging to Derek, despite all that he did, probably had in it a marital element. I was like a wife who will put up with anything in order to save the marriage.

I considered going to a shrink, but all the shrinks I had ever met in a social way had been so dull and flat, so unshakable in their self-esteem. Instead I talked to friends; sometimes I would call Agatha in San Francisco. Once I said to her—very insightfully, I thought: "You know, when a man is really treating me badly I'm afraid to leave him; he might do something worse."

"Well, I *guess* that makes sense."

At another time, a rather coarse friend, a man, an unsuccessful writer, said to me, "You know, Daphne, you remind me of a man who puts on a tuxedo to take a crap." I didn't quite understand that, but I caught the drift.

I was, however, finally on the verge of leaving Derek when he craftily suggested a trip to Paris.

Six days in Paris!

He had business there; of course his business was the real reason for our trip, something to do with the Common Market, but still— We would have all our evenings together there: perhaps Paris would magically transform us?

I told Derek that I would much rather stay on the Left Bank, and although he said that he rather fancied the George V, we compromised on the Lutetia, Boulevard Raspail—a little too grand for me, and not quite grand enough for him, as things turned out.

On the plane going over, high above the Atlantic, over his third vodka, true to form, Derek remarked, "One thing I do like about you, Daphne, my girl, is that you're not a child. Younger women—their problems—lamentable." *La*mentable, accent on the first syllable.

He had been having trouble with a younger woman? Well, obviously so. And despite the number of times he had done precisely this to me before, that thought lodged itself within me like a barb. My response was Pavlovian, or something even more stupid.

Then, as we circled the hedge-crossed fields, the red-tiled country rooftops of France, Derek asked me if I had ever known anyone with a strong Southern accent. "Impossible to understand," he said.

A very young Southern woman. Jesus Christ.

Nevertheless, there was Paris, gray and lovely, strangled

in traffic, reeking of fumes—and poignantly, piercingly familiar. Or was I simply pierced with pain from Derek? At that moment it was hard to tell.

As we dressed for dinner, he remarked that he had noticed I did not go in for black lace underthings. He found them attractive, rather.

Why in hell didn't you bring your young Southern twat in her black lace skivvies instead of me? Why do I have to hear this stuff? I was silently screaming all that at Derek, although I could never have managed to bring out those words; they would have sounded crazy, or so I thought.

At dinner, Lucas-Carton, which was terribly posh and formal—not a good choice—for some reason I told Derek a very modified version of my history with Jean-Paul. Maybe in a feeble way I was trying to get back at him; if so, that was a total failure. An observation: people are never jealous when you want them to be, only when you do not. What Derek said was "Well, just as well you can't see him now, I'm sure. Those middle-class Frenchmen always run to fat, and they get bald early on. You may have even passed each other in the street."

Of course this was long before I had heard anything about the present Jean-Paul, although I somehow knew that he could be neither bald nor fat. Nor, for that matter, could he ever have been described as middle-class. But I was too depressed, too beaten down to argue. And I was certainly too low-spirited to think of trying to get in touch with Jean-Paul on that trip.

I didn't even call Ellie Osborne, although I knew from Agatha that she was there.

I walked through streets that once had been familiar, and loved; I went to the Louvre, Notre Dame, Sainte-Chapelle. I stood on Pont Neuf and regarded the river. I had a solitary drink on the terrace of the Flore, where once I

had shared a beer with Jean-Paul. An attractive blond man—
a Dane, perhaps, some sort of Scandinavian—tried manfully
to pick me up, with nice smiles, bright white teeth and sea-
blue eyes, but I wasn't equal to anything like that, not then.

Derek and I got back late on a Tuesday afternoon; he
rushed up to Boston—to see his young black-laced Southern
friend is what I assumed. Alone in my apartment, I unpacked
and bathed, and lay down for a nap. I was incredibly tired.

I woke up at some strange pre-dawn hour, completely
out of touch with time, with my place on the globe. I felt as
an alcoholic woman must feel, waking and not sure how she
got into that bed, nor what day it was.

And I wondered, How *had* I got into such a situation,
so skewered with pain, impaled on jealous thrusts from an
inconsiderate, really cruel man?

Crazy: it would be as crazy to continue with Derek as
it would be for that lost alcoholic to go on drinking. I simply
would not. I would give him up. Break off, cut out. Never
mind that I should have done this months ago, clearly.

And the next day, miraculously—God liked me, after all
—Agatha called and told me about her house in California. I
know that I would have broken off with Derek anyway—I
really was ready to—but knowing his sort of perversity, I was
sure that he would have made it as difficult as possible,
mightily exercising himself to keep me around. A strong excuse for getting out of town, all the way to California, was
a tremendous help.

Agatha had saved me.

4

For my first couple of weeks in San Francisco, then, I walked about and looked at the city; I spent time with Agatha—I moped about Jean-Paul, and gave a few angry backward thoughts in the direction of Derek. And I thought about the house surrounding me, trying to see what I could make of it, what shape it would take, what forms and colors.

One morning, as I was contemplating the kitchen in that speculative way, someone rang the doorbell.

I went to answer it, and there on the stoop was a very tall, very blond young man, in what looked like old army clothes, faded green. His long white-blond hair was pulled back into a sort of ponytail, tied with a thong; a moustache and a full beard covered a lot of his face.

He introduced himself. "I'm Royce Houston." And he handed me a card, using his left hand, from which two fingers were missing. He was a carpenter, he said, and so his card announced. In case I was thinking about any remodeling.

At first, for a moment, this seemed an answer to some telepathic summons, but then I realized that it was of course a clever, not too farfetched calculation on Royce Houston's part: the house had recently changed hands; new owners often remodeled. He would have just been waiting around, watching me. Choosing what seemed a propitious moment.

His smile too looked calculated, a quick gesture that did not match his eyes, which were distant and vaguely hostile. "I'm staying with my folks, out at Stinson Beach, temporarily," he told me. "So if you call there, ask for Whitey. I'm called that, inevitably. The old man's named Royce too." The "inevitably" had been as jarring, as off-key as his smile, and infinitely condescending. Toward me? Toward his parents? In fact he was a little scarey, Whitey Houston was: shell-shocked, a Vietnam vet? On drugs of some sort? I was sure that I would never call him, but of course I took his card and thanked him—and was treated to another quick hostile smile.

I was very glad to see him go. That encounter had shaken me up, and in a businesslike way I tried to concentrate on the kitchen.

I thought that I would create a central island, butcher-blocked: a small sink, chopping areas, a chute for garbage. And around the walls of the room I would have some banquettes made, upholstered in a bright sturdy fabric that would cost the earth and look very simple and inexpensive.

But I was still unnerved, not quite concentrating, and so next I went out for a walk, out into the lovely clear fall weather, in my beautiful corner of the city, overlooking the Bay. In that neighborhood I was constantly riveted by some sudden blue vista of that Bay, glimpsed from some broad space between the imposing houses, or from the top of a wide descending street. Blue water, white sails and often a big white liner, pushing out toward the Golden Gate, or a tanker, coming in.

The architecture of that particular neighborhood interested me much less. Except for a few imaginative departures, the houses were standard upper-class fare, massive and bulky, totally lacking in grace. And the people on those streets also looked familiar enough: the suburban affluent of the middle

Seventies; lots of expensive boots and imported denim, good sweaters and English raincoats. Large women out walking little dogs. Joggers, smartly outfitted. Kids on skateboards or bikes.

That morning I noticed a thin pretty woman with short gray hair and large, dark, very sad eyes, out walking a small and lively dog. I wondered if she could possibly be the woman whose husband was shot. As we passed each other, I smiled, intending friendliness, but she looked away. Her dog was a short-haired, nutty-looking mutt, frisking ridiculously—a promiscuous sniffer. He rushed up to me and I bent down and patted him, and then the woman turned around and smiled: two dog lovers, acknowledging each other. I very much hoped that she was not the one whose husband was killed, but I felt that she was.

Back home in Agatha's house, I decided that one long window could be made into a French door, leading out onto a small deck, among those beautiful old trees, in the California sun.

That night I had an angry, drunken call from Derek, accusing me of irrationality, of craziness—as he usually did. Agatha would never pay me, he predicted; friends never did. I would come back more broke than ever, the implication being that poverty would return me to Derek. And "Just don't count on my being around for your return," he admonished.

"Derek, I wouldn't think of it," I promised, hanging up.

But I felt grateful to him, really, for behaving so badly, reminding me of all his worst qualities. "Getting over" Derek had been much easier than I could have hoped.

Leaving the telephone, I went over to my improvised desk, in the space where the kitchen table would be, and I wrote a longish letter to Ellie Osborne in Paris, whose address I had got from Agatha. And I asked her, in passing, if perhaps she had ever heard of the famous economic theorist, the Socialist writer Jean-Paul ————.

5

On the way to Stinson Beach, the following Sunday, I
told Agatha about my short visit from Whitey Houston.

Before I had even finished the story, I noticed that she
was looking at me oddly, her sidewise look. And so I knew
what she would say almost before she could get it out: "That's
where we're going today, to the Houstons'," she said.
"They're friends of mine. Whitey's parents."

But I don't want to meet them, I started to say, and then
did not. I just said, "Well."

Agatha gave a short laugh. "You're right," she said. "It's
an awfully small town. You'll get used to this kind of coincidence." And she added, "You're right about Whitey,
though. You wouldn't get along with him."

We were driving then over the steep green and perilous
hills of Marin County, north of the bridge. At intervals one
side of the road would drop away into a cavernous gorge;
there were spectacular views of further rolling green deep-
valleyed hills that literally took your breath away, they were
so vast and beautiful. And with anyone else at the wheel I
would have been nervous—Derek always drove his Porsche
maniacally; he and I would never have made it over these
hills. But with Agatha I felt and knew myself to be absolutely safe: she was blessed.

As she drove, she told me a little about the Houstons, who were to figure so largely in my life, who were to become, for me, *the* Californians.

Ruth Houston, Whitey's mother, was a lawyer; like Agatha, she had been a Sixties political activist, which was how they knew each other. There were two children, Whitey and his slightly older sister, Caroline. The two kids had always got along well, great friends, but there had always been trouble, real trouble, between Ruth and her son Whitey. This hit a sort of peak, family fights and scenes, during the Vietnam war. Whitey was all for it: get in there, kill, win. So he volunteered and went to war, and Ruth went off marching and organizing for peace.

I asked about the other two, Whitey's father and the girl.

When Agatha is unsure of what she's saying, or feels in some way uneasy, her voice tightens, as it did now. "That was never quite clear," she said. "My feeling was that they both pretty much agreed with Ruth, although neither of them is really political, and they're both really crazy about Whitey. At first those two, Royce and Caroline, kept out of it, out of the fights as much as they could, but then it was too late and Whitey was gone."

We were coming out of a dark grove of trees, pine and fir and eucalyptus, redwoods and huge bay trees, and then suddenly, beyond open green sloping fields, there was the sea —that day a dazzling blue, glinting sunlight.

"When Whitey came back, he'd changed his mind, of course," Agatha said. "I guess he had a pretty awful time."

"Unlike other people who loved it there."

We both laughed, although a little uneasily—trying for our old brand of black wit.

Determinedly she went on; it was somehow necessary to prepare me for the Houstons. "Anyway," she said, "they seem to have patched things up somehow. Although Ruth seems—I don't know—even more changed than Whitey is. Not adjusting to the Seventies." This last of course was heavily ironic.

I asked what the father, Royce Houston, did.

Again that tight voice. "Well, not much, and I guess that's something of a problem. Ruth is a maniac about work. What's that dumb new word—'workaholic'? Royce made a lot of money in real estate, a while back, and since then he's sort of dabbled." Her voice tighter yet, she added, "He's very attractive."

I thought, Ah, poor Agatha; she's in love with the husband of a friend. How unlike her.

We had reached the sea, and we turned right and drove on past a cluster of somewhat shabby gray-shingled houses, sprawling and divergent in shape and size. Then a crossroads, a stoplight and stores. A mile or so later we turned left onto a dirt road, beside smaller, shabbier houses that at intervals blocked our view of the sea.

On the other side of the road was a long lagoon, flat and quiescent, surrounded by huge clumps of wild pampas grass, and weeds. Seabirds gathered there in scattered groups.

We stopped at a gate, and Agatha gave the guard the Houstons' name, and we were admitted to a "development" of obviously very expensive, design-controlled, close-together houses. At last we stopped at one of the largest, on the ocean side—a huge house, really, with shining areas of glass. We parked there, Agatha's old VW among the new German or English or Italian sports cars; we got out and walked toward the open front patio of the house.

Agatha had seemed to be telling me a lot about the Houstons; I had felt well prepared for them, maybe over-prepared, but as two very tall, blond and extremely hand-some people came out toward us from the patio, I thought:

How strange of her not to say that Ruth is a tall blonde beauty, as well as an activist lawyer. Why didn't she say how *sexy* those two people are?

Well, how like her not to, really, was my second thought; Agatha doesn't think in terms of sex and beauty.

But then we were introduced, and it turned out that although the man was indeed Royce Houston, father of Whitey —they looked considerably alike—the tall blonde woman, in pink clothes, was called Stacy something.

Why do some people look so clearly sexual, so that you react to them instantly in that way? Obvious physical characteristics aside, I think they look sexy because that is what is on their minds.

Royce was not only large—very: about six five—and blond and good-looking, green-eyed, his smile was very sexy. Whereas I would have guessed that his son, who was not sexy-looking, had mainly hostile thoughts.

Stacy looked sexy too, at least at that moment; otherwise hers was a rather vacuous face—it could and did quite easily go blank. I found that I disliked her in an instant primitive way, which at first I took to be pure sexual jealousy; she was so much what I was not—blonde and small-breasted, with an overall look of smooth perfection that was quite unachievable for me, even had I ever tried. She was probably stupid-shrewd, I thought, and I consigned her to that alimony-rich group of divorcées whom I had recognized in other places, women who are getting so much alimony that they have to marry upward, as it were. In the meantime they use gay men for escorts and married men for sex. Like most clandestine lovers, she and Royce had no idea how obvious their connection was, to anyone; they may even have thought that a public show of friendliness would be misleading. And I thought again, Oh, poor Agatha.

Ruth Houston, whom we met once we got inside the house, was quite a surprise, a most curious match for Royce: a small dark woman, with large unhappy eyes and a tight clenched mouth. I thought she even looked a little crazy, desperate. She wore a gaudy orange cotton caftan that did nothing to brighten her look.

And I met a quantity of other people, crowding that large, dramatically beamed and windowed room, half open to a long view of dunes, the sea. Everyone was very dressed up, in a way that people I knew in the East had not been, not for years; in fact I was more conscious of all those clothes than of the people. I could have been looking at a room full of mannequins, in their leather and silk and velvet, their silver Indian jewelry, their mid-Seventies opulence.

The food, too, already laid out on a long bandanna-clothed table, was also predictably opulent: the crab and white wine, varieties of quiches, the tray of tiny pastries for dessert.

It was really depressing, all those smiling laughing eating people, in all those clothes, behaving as though they were doing something important. Lonely is probably what I actually felt, but lonely for any particular person? Surely not for Derek—for Jean-Paul? More likely it was simple loneliness, that of a woman too unused to being alone.

Agatha and I never talked in an explicit way about her love affairs; I just assumed that she sometimes had them. Generally I talked about mine, and she listened. Once, though, I do remember saying to her, during some particularly ill-advised affair of my own—maybe when it had finally become clear to me that Jacob was hopelessly on heroin: a junkie—and at a time when it seemed to me that all the women I knew were involved in some sort of bad love affairs, then I said to Agatha that there seemed to be an inverse relationship between the intelligence of women and their choice of men. To which Agatha quickly answered, "Well, in that case I must be a genius." We laughed a lot at that, true and unfunny as it was.

Now that I was seeing her on home ground, I wondered: Would I hear more about her lovers, maybe meet them? Were any of them in this room, right now? Given that particular rather homogeneous group, it seemed unlikely, but then so did Royce Houston, even as the object of a "crush" of Agatha's.

Agatha looked less out of place with those people than I would have expected, however. In her neat Levis and dark blue turtleneck she looked simply young, and rather old-fashioned.

Ruth Houston, in her own house, looked very out of place. The bright caftan was all wrong; it might once have been becoming, at some other and perhaps happier time of her life—not now. I assumed that she must be unhappy about Royce and big blonde Stacy, but if she was she seemed remarkably unaware of them. Normally I would have felt a sort of female-bonding sympathy for Ruth, but she looked as angry as she did unhappy, and when she forgot my name for the third time trying to introduce me to someone—How many people does she know named Daphne? I wondered—I decided that she was a worse than indifferent hostess, and I wasn't really interested in her problems.

And maybe I let this hostility of Ruth Houston's serve as an excuse, for normally I am not at all drawn to other women's husbands, or their lovers, and I have to admit: at first I was powerfully drawn to Royce Houston, despite Ruth, and Stacy, and even Agatha's possible feelings. I wondered what he did all day. I wanted him to notice me in some way.

While coffee was being served, by a trio of handsome young blond men in red jackets, yet another good-looking young couple arrived, hurrying through the patio and into the living room, laughing, seemingly delighted with each other. At first glance one would surely have taken them for lovers. A tall blond young man, a much smaller, darker girl. But then I recognized the man: it was Whitey, but all dressed up in something suède.

Royce went over to greet his son—enthusiastically, hugging his shoulders, obviously crazy about his boy—and then he hugged the girl, and I heard him say, "Ah, Caroline. You got here."

So—the young couple were Whitey and his sister Caroline, not lovers. Caroline looked very like her mother, small and dark, but she was much happier, more attractive than her mother was, although with something wistful in her eyes. And I thought how strange the genes were in that family. Sexist genes: the large blond beauty all going unfairly to the men.

How strongly, too, they all felt about each other, Royce and his son and daughter! Did Ruth, the mother, feel left out? Powerful feelings were visible in their very postures as they stood there together for a minute. Caroline seemed to adore her father and her brother; that was on her face when she looked from one to the other of those men, their similar handsome faces—similar except for Whitey's moustache and beard. And Royce adored both his kids. Did Whitey "adore" anyone? His face, as he looked at his sister and responded to something she had said, bespoke amusement and affection, maybe some stronger feeling too. I got no sense of how he felt about his father.

I was introduced to the kids, and it was soon clear both that Whitey remembered me very well and that he did not

like me at all. Quite possibly, of course, he had sensed what
I felt about him; I certainly did not trust him—not at all.

Caroline and I liked each other very much, on sight. It
was the sort of affinity that women sometimes feel toward
each other—Agatha and I; I guess men too. It is not at all
like "falling in love," there being no sense of dizziness, of
doom. Caroline said that she had heard I was doing Agatha's
house, how nice. She lived not far away from me, she said,
out on Clement Street. She had a studio where she did sculptures in wool. I had seen some things of that sort in New
York, and found them interesting. She said that I should
come out to see her; have tea. There were some nice Russian
tearooms out there, she said.

Good, I'd like that, I told her.

That day Caroline was wearing a sweater she must have
made: very coarse, irregular wool, colors from natural to
yellow to pale orange. Becoming to her hair, and her sun-
brown skin. She had what is called an "interesting" face—
meaning, I guess, more intelligent than pretty.

Something about me at that moment seemed to have
caught Royce Houston's attention. His son's hostility? Caroline's affection? My height? Impossible to tell. But he came
over and said that he thought I hadn't seen his study: would
I like to?

Yes, I would.

He opened a door to a flight of stairs, leading down. I
followed his broad shoulders, narrow waist, tight Levi's over
a very handsome ass. Such a huge man, hard not to think
about the size of his cock. I must have been a little tipsy,
too, all that nervously gulped white wine. Dizzily, I imagined
hot embraces.

At the bottom of the stairs, Royce turned and took my
hand, and though I did not lurch against him, I am sure he

must have seen lust written all over my face—seen, and dismissed it. For which I never quite forgave him. He could have spared a Sunday afternoon kiss, I thought.

He said, not looking at me, "It's kind of an interesting room, don't you think?"

All that was interesting about it was its situation; it had somehow been carved down from the beach, so that it seemed to be at water level. Otherwise, it was perfectly nice but in no way remarkable. But someone, Agatha, or Ruth, must have told him that I was a decorator, and he wanted me to see his room, the fruit of his idle richness.

Trying not to feel put down, trying to focus on that boring room, I next saw that it contained a remarkable number of jungle animals, lions, some zebras on the run, an obscene rhinoceros. Too many animals, and all of them too large.

Going from one photograph to another, which seemed the sensible, the expected thing to do, I tried to cope with my feelings of rejection. Turned on by Royce, I would have expected him to feel the same. So far it had generally been like that for me. God knows I was not everyone's cup of tea, so to speak, but then neither was everyone mine. And I wondered: Was this the way it was going to be from now on? Have I reached an age to be turned down by men of my own age?

"I shot all these myself," Royce was saying, which restored a little reality to my musings, the reality of irritation: a strong bias against hunting, guns, people who do all that. I asked, "You hunt a lot?"

"Oh, no." He sounded appalled, and quite as priggish as I must have sounded. "With my camera. I like to photograph animals. I go on camera safaris. East Africa. Next time I'm trying to persuade Ruth and the kids to come along."

"Oh."

"And here's my house at Tahoe," he was saying. "It doesn't look like much, but it's really beautiful."

He showed me a picture of a small, entirely ordinary house, and I exclaimed, because he seemed to expect it—and because there had begun to seem something rather touching in his thus exhibiting his treasures—"Oh, how nice," I said, examining the picture of a small house. Not knowing that I was to spend the happiest week of my life in that house, though not with Royce.

"Well," Royce said, "I guess we'd better get back to the others."

We went upstairs; we re-entered the party and no one looked at us with anything like suspicion.

Later, coming out of the bathroom, I encountered my hostess, Ruth Houston. She was standing at the mirror in a bedroom, combing her short brown hair with a total lack of interest. She was escaping from her own party, and she didn't care who knew it.

I said that I liked her house.

"Well, it's much more important to Royce than it is to me," she remarked. "He's from very poor people—Okies, really—and he cares about spending a lot of money. Boats, safaris, cars. My folks weren't rich but they were richer than his were. I think it makes a difference."

This longish speech had not really been directed to me; it could have been just something that she said to people sometimes. And so an assenting murmur seemed sufficient. Intimate revelations from people I'm not close to make me uncomfortable. But she had struck a familiar, nostalgic note: she reminded me of certain women from my Wisconsin childhood, women who would just say whatever was on their minds, in a free, frank way.

I muttered something ambiguous in response, and Ruth went on with her hair. And I wondered again if she felt left out, with all that intense feeling running between her husband and children. Not to mention Stacy.

When I came back into the main room, there indeed was Stacy, and she was talking in a hyper-animated way to Whitey. They were across the room from me; in the continuing din I had no idea what they were saying, but their two postures said a lot. Stacy was in perpetual motion, gesturing with everything—her eyebrows, hands, hips, legs; arching her back so that her breasts pointed straight out. And Whitey watched her; absolutely still, he had a slightly passive smile. And I had an evil thought about how passive he must be in bed, waiting to be pleased.

Then a small and pretty young man, a decorator to whom I had earlier been introduced, went over to Stacy and Whitey, and extracted Stacy, who was apparently his date. Time to go home.

Agatha came up to me and said that she thought it was time to go. She looked exhausted, and harried; I understood then that having me along was supposed to have made the party easier for her; I should have been a sort of buffer against her strong feelings about that difficult, maybe impossible family.

I agreed that yes, we certainly should leave.

6

I know: this year when a woman feels nervously horny
—and this year it's perfectly okay for a woman to be
horny—she is supposed to get a vibrator, masturbate and at
least to think about making it with another woman. But suppose you aren't turned on at all in a sexual way by women,
including yourself?

That describes my own condition; I simply did not want
to do any of those things. I was not even sure that I could.

Many shrinks, and many feminists too, of course, would
say that this is a lack in me—a gap in my instincts, as it were.
Still, nevertheless, I do not believe in forcing things of that
nature. I don't think you should do anything that you don't
want to do in bed, either to please another person or for
theoretical reasons.

A much-married man, an aging Liberal I had once known
in New York, told me he felt that he should have a sexual
relationship with a black man—he *should*, for political reasons. To me that sounded ridiculous.

Well, my inhibitions left me sexually bound to men, and
sometimes I ended up with near-psychopaths: Jake the junkie,
mean Derek. On the other hand that's really no excuse; I'm
sure that lots of women with my same sexual bent have life-
times of pleasant lovers, or even a nice husband or so. But

whatever had led me and tied me for a while to Derek, the experience had been scarey, as well as cautionary. And so, the day after the party at the Houstons', I began to think that it was probably lucky, Royce's not being taken with me. For all I knew, he could turn out to be as mean as Derek was; also, confused as I was in my feelings about Ruth, it was still a lousy thing to do to another woman. Ruth certainly had enough trouble without me in her life.

The real truth was that I knew it was time, high time, to get along for a while without an ongoing love affair. To concentrate on work, and friendships. Read, get a lot of exercise. Not brood about Jean-Paul, or anyone.

Let absent or dead lovers rest in peace.

7

Like so much else in San Francisco, Jackson Square, the center for decorators, antique dealers, fabric houses, was at first glance both original and exceptionally attractive: a few blocks of pleasantly restored, nice old brick buildings, freshly painted Victorian wood. Nothing over three stories high. A closed-off mall for strollers, meanderers. Trees, and flower boxes of geraniums or marguerites. Big glass windows that displayed appealing wares, old brass and well-designed new furniture.

And then, with a harder look, it all became sadly familiar. I had seen those same strolling couples before, the peacock men in tight-fitting, light-shaded clothes, the dowdy, too heavy women with red alcoholic faces, in double-knit suits. I recognized them as my *confrères*, my colleagues, the local decorators. Their clients, too, fell into recognizable categories: the elderly rich, looking somehow Midwestern, and dazzled by it all; and the stylishly thin, recently well-divorced young women. I had even seen all that furniture before, in showrooms in New York and Boston, and Washington, D.C. And as for the restoration itself, the more I looked the less novel it became. It was simply smaller and prettier than other such efforts, in other cities, as San Francisco itself is a small and pretty city.

In New York I have methods of avoiding this depressing scene: I visit and buy from mills in Lebanon, New Hampshire—in recent years I would then detour to Boston for a visit, of sorts, with Derek. And I have a crazy infallible genius of a cabinetmaker in Hackensack. Since so many of my clients have been broke friends, this has worked out well. They appreciate my efforts.

But there I was in San Francisco, with that huge house of Agatha's, and all that money. And how ironic it was that the General's money should in that sense have come to me: so often I had wondered how on earth he came by it, and none of my speculations had been at all flattering to him, the mean old bastard. I felt plunged into an unfamiliar and vastly overpriced—in fact a crazily costly—world, hitherto only glimpsed at infrequent intervals. In Jackson Square, all around me there were people spending enormous sums of money, and they were very serious about all that spending; they felt that it was the right thing to do, and they *cared* about what they bought, and owned, and displayed.

In the year that I spent in San Francisco, I was never to make any excursion without running across some person whom I had seen or met or heard of before; that day, across the street, I saw Stacy, of the Houston party. She was again with that pretty young man—her decorator, I guess. Her tall thin blonde body was, as always, in constant motion, but that day she seemed to be miming petulance; assuming they were having the kind of decorator-client quarrel that I knew about, I found it easy to avoid them. And I thought, Thank heaven she's not my client; I know her type, restless and greedy, in a random, indecisive way.

*

The high point of my trip to Jackson Square was my discovery that my favorite line of linen had its headquarters a few blocks from there, unlike Brunschwig & Fils, Schumacher, et cetera, whose main office and showrooms are in New York. The Henry Calvin building, then, contained more beautiful linen samples than I could have imagined—perfect for Agatha, who is, like me, a linen freak. Even the company's nice brick building had an old-world quality of excellence, of care. I spent a happy forty-five or fifty minutes there, marveling at beautiful fabrics—before I moved on to the shocking end of my day.

What happened was: when I got home, after one instant I knew that someone had been there. Someone had broken in, had been all over the house.

First off, I saw that my mail was piled up on the hall table. It had not yet arrived when I went out that morning; eager to hear from Ellie anything about Jean-Paul, I was highly aware of mail. Someone had picked up and neatly stacked my letters, which struck me as a most curious gesture, taking in your victim's mail. But this was a most curious break-in, all around.

I suppose that by now almost everyone who lives in a city has been in some way robbed—houses broken into, cars stolen, been mugged in a familiar parking lot or an elevator—but so far none of it had happened to me, just the garbage can my second day in that house. Going through all the downstairs rooms, and then the upstairs, I began to experience the emotions that I had heard about so often from my robbed friends—a vicarious *déjà vu*, as it were. I felt both angry and afraid—it occurred to me that the person might still be there, in the house, although I was fairly sure that he was not. And I experienced a sense of violation, not exactly like being raped

—I guess: that hasn't happened to me either, not yet—but still a terrible sense of having been entirely, nakedly exposed to an unknown, hostile person.

In the kitchen the small portable TV was missing, along with my electric typewriter. Well, of course those would be the obvious things to take. Nothing else there gone, that I could see.

Upstairs, in the big bedroom where I was more or less camping out, I began to look through drawers, in the closet, and that is where my strong sense of defilement began: the person had been through literally everything I owned, and had chosen what to take with a keenly, most snobbishly selective eye. Gone were my few good silk blouses; I was left with synthetics. The same with sweaters: cashmere missing, lamb's wool still in its place. Skirts and dresses—again, the good ones were gone. Even the few scarves and gloves that I had brought to California had been gone through, thinned out. It was hard not to feel in this a strong element of personal dislike, as though the ripper-offer had rebuked me for not having *all* good things. I tried to dismiss those feelings as a kind of situational paranoia, and I remembered—usefully —that several ripped-off friends had said they felt the same.

Another thing friends had said was that you could not be sure what was missing for several days; things from time to time would turn up gone, and so it was with me. In the meantime I telephoned Agatha.

Afternoons are when she sees patients, of course; she is apt to be extremely busy. But for once she seemed not to be. She listened, and she said she would call her insurance person, which I hadn't even thought of. She would call me back.

Ten minutes later she did call, and she was chuckling to herself. "It's kind of unbelievable," she said. "I took out a policy on that house, and sort of without my knowing it they added a rider that covers you completely. It's really funny: usually people think they're covered and they're not."

"God must love you."

"I should hope so, all the time I give Him." And then she told me what I already knew, to make a list of what I had lost, but not for several days. To call the police and make a report.

Of course I felt considerably better; for a manic moment I even considered pretending to losses that I had not sustained, claiming jewelry and furs that I had never owned. And maybe if Agatha had not been involved I would have. Agatha is the most moral living Episcopalian; she does not believe in cheating anyone at all, whereas if I could get away with it I would love to cheat an insurance company, an oil company—or the I.R.S., for that matter.

But it was still depressing, the idea of someone's having come in and poked about among my things. I still felt it as a sort of personal attack. Why me, I thought. I wondered if someone had been watching me, checking my habits of arrival and departure, maybe deciding that he or she—I had to admit, it could have been a woman—did not like me, that I deserved to be ripped off. The only clear fact about the breaker-in was that it was a person of taste, with a good eye for quality. But maybe these days all robbers are discriminating.

Discouraged, and a little scared, I went back upstairs, and it was then that I discovered my favorite earrings gone, big very plain wide silver hoops. Real silver, by some standards not expensive, but much more than I usually pay for earrings. And they were certainly not unique; I was sure that I could find their duplicates in some good San Francisco store. But the thought of buying them again was deeply, if irrationally depressing. Emblematic, I guess those earrings were.

That night, as I was making my dietetic dinner for one, steak tartare, which I had planned to season with some imported soy sauce from Cost Plus, I saw that the soy sauce was missing from its shelf. At that point all the emotions that I had felt about being robbed united in a single flare of rage. Chopping onions, crying over them, I muttered all the obscene words I could think of. Which didn't make me feel much better either.

The next day I dutifully called the police and made my report, and a week later I made an honest list of my losses and handed it to Agatha.

8

I did not exactly keep to my resolution involving not brooding about old love affairs; in fact, as usual I thought of little else—after all, to what else, so far, had my life been dedicated? And I wondered, sometimes, just how it had all begun, this nutty obsessiveness with love and men. A shrink would tie it to my father's early death, I guess, but I rather thought that my mania began with my Uncle Don, with whom I fell in love when I was five, the year my father died.

My mother went down to Palm Beach to recover—at that time a quiet, cheap resort—and I was sent from Madison, where we lived, to Frederick, a small town in Iowa, where actually I had been born, but I hardly knew the town. And, staying there with my stately grandparents, I fell in love with my Uncle Don, the husband of my father's sister Margaret. Don was a perfectly nice, rather ordinary young man in his middle twenties, with a round, prematurely bald head, wide flaring ears and small irregular teeth. Toward him I behaved so terribly, with such consistent brattiness, that he could not have suspected love to be its cause. Besides, whoever heard of a five-year-old in love? Certainly not Don.

About my father's death I understood very little, and it is possible that no one tried to explain; how could they? In any case, I was sad and shy and embarrassed, and deeply puzzled. Dead? No one else's father had died, why mine? What was pneumonia? I am sure that my grandparents were saddened by their inability to communicate anything of what they felt to me, along with their natural grief at the death of a much-loved son.

Their household seems eccentric now; not so to any right-thinking person of that time. Simply, my grandfather had married a woman with three unmarried sisters, all of whom he supported in a small house attached to the rear of his own. From this distance it is hard to work out their ages, but since my parents were in their thirties when I was born, all those people would have been somewhere in their sixties. To me they seemed simply old—Old People, like those encountered in myths and fairy stories, and in the Bible.

And then there were Margaret and Don, younger than my parents; but they were still grown-ups, much older than I was. And their baby, Peggy, who was too young for me to think about.

My grandfather was my favorite of that aged group; to me he seemed both kind and reliable. He was the one who taught me to roller-skate, having decided that the old ladies of the house were much too frail for that task, and Margaret was too busy with her baby. In fact the grandmother and her sisters were all rather nervous and subject to headaches, fits of irritation.

Across a tidy space of lawn from my grandfather's decorous and shiningly white house, and sharing the box-wood that separated it from the sidewalk, was a smaller, narrower, yellow house; Aunt Margaret and Uncle Don lived there, with baby Peggy. Margaret, in her twenties, was a beautiful dark young woman, warmly and sensuously in love with her husband, who was truly in love with her. Bald Don. Margaret was thin, heavy-breasted.

Don was an engineer, out of work in his profession—this was in 1940, just before the booming years of war. He had taken a job in a nearby cellophane factory. That winter we all, every evening just at four-thirty, ceremoniously went out to fetch him from the factory, in my grandfather's dignified Chevrolet. I can still recall the smell of that factory, which was horrible but was mingled with my wild emotion at the prospect of seeing Don.

Every morning all of us assembled in the parlor for morning prayers, the grandparents and the great-aunts, and me. Don and Margaret were excused from this ritual, probably because of his job, which everyone respected, and Margaret's baby, whom they all foolishly—to my jealous mind— adored.

On weekdays I was driven to school after breakfast by Stuart, the black chauffeur, who also drove Uncle Don out to the factory. The school was private, a few children in a house in a not very good part of town. I did not exactly make friends there. We were all rather young for real friendships, and also I was very aware of my temporary status: Frederick was not where I lived, and those children's accents were strange, whereas at home in Madison there were people I had always known; I imagined that I always would.

And, more important, my attention was so passionately focused on my surrounding world of adults that I had little emotional energy left for other children, perhaps even interest in them. School was simply a filler for my days, and bridged the hours until it was time to go and get Uncle Don.

But why, each evening that winter in Frederick, did all of us arrange ourselves in my grandfather's car and drive out to the cellophane factory to fetch Uncle Don from work? Stuart could perfectly well have gone by himself, or Stuart and my grandfather. But no, we all went—all except the great-aunts, who stayed at home to take care of adorable little Peggy—every workday at four-thirty, in order to be there when the factory whistle blew at five. Quite possibly my grandfather thought our massed and dignified presence would somehow compensate for the indignity of Don's job; I now think that must have been it.

Grandfather sat beside Stuart, up in the front seat; my grandmother and Margaret and I sat in the back.

When Don came out of the factory and walked over to where we were, and got in the back seat, I would move over to my grandmother's lap, or Margaret's.

EXCEPT: one night Don got into the car, and kissed Margaret, as he always did, and then he said, "Gosh, honey, you look tired. Here, let me take Daphne."

And so that night we drove home through an exceptionally vivid scarlet sunset, with me perched dizzyingly on Don's strong hard knees. Once he said, with a small indulgent chuckle, "Just relax, Daphne. Try to take it easy." Words that I was to hear quite often, later in life. Wanting badly to lean back against him, to relax, instead I bounced as hard as I could, up and down, until he cried out, "That's enough! Daphne, cut it out!"

Did that circumstance ever recur? I cannot remember, but I do recall my wild hopes that it might; on any evening Don might say to Margaret, "Honey, you look tired. I'll take Daphne."

And toward that small hope, involving that little possibility of pleasure, I directed all my days, my waking hours.

*

Many years later, as a just-divorced young woman, I was involved with a man who was married, who was rarely free to see me. And it came to me at last, without my consciously thinking of Don and of those meager old hopes, that those few enchanted hours were not really worth the weeks and months of waiting, of waste.

Without exactly knowing how, I was aware of being considered "difficult" that year. The problem may have been that I was living with people who were more than half a century older than I was. In any case, at some point generous Margaret must have said to her mother and father, "You all look just plain exhausted. You let us take Daphne over here for a while. . . . Why, no, it won't be the least bit of trouble."

And that is when I began to be truly terrible.

At dinner I played with my food, staring at Uncle Don, and sometimes, if no one noticed that I wasn't eating, I would make distorted, ludicrous faces, until helplessly Don would shout, "Daphne, for God's sake, eat your dinner! We're almost ready for dessert."

Or, I wouldn't be ready when Stuart came to take Don to the factory and me to school.

Once, at dinner, when Don had been urging me somewhat more strongly than usual to finish my chicken and rice, whatever, so that dessert could be served, I said to him, on an uncontrollable sudden impulse, in a loud cold voice, "You shut up, you damn fool."

Well.

After a literally stunned silence, mild-mannered Don began to shout: "You little brat, you go upstairs this minute!" How often, before, he must have longed to shout exactly that.

And so, terrified of what I had done, and giddily excited by his aroused attention, I went upstairs alone to bed, and quite probably I cried, my melodramatic self-pity at last justified. And later Aunt Margaret came up with a plate of dessert and comforting words, and an admonition that Don worked hard and got very tired. We must all be considerate.

Did Don and Margaret worry that their darling little Peggy would turn out to be like me? Unlikely that they did; such a thing would not have seemed possible to them, and they probably all blamed my bad character on my mother, whose intelligence provoked suspicion among them.

And about Peggy they were quite right, of course: the last time I saw her, in New York, she had made a superb dinner for a dozen people, a Thanksgiving dinner (and how like her to invite me, a stray and disreputable cousin, known for too many love affairs), despite having one arm in a cast from a skiing accident. Despite the demands of three very small children. Even her husband is nice. Needless to say, I rarely see them.

Don found his tiny daughter perfect and beautiful, even when she screamed and spit and made those appalling smells —those were the things that I noticed exclusively: how could he love little Peggy?

And he lovingly helped Margaret with the baby's care. I used to watch, astounded and deeply agitated, as Don bathed Peggy in her canvas Bathinette, holding her so gently, soaping her everywhere, then rinsing, lifting her from the water and patting the pink flesh dry, powdering her chubby buttocks and between her legs—*how could he?*

Surprising, I think, that more children are not murdered by other children.

On one bright winter afternoon, Don decided to take us sledding—all of us, Margaret, Peggy and me—out near the Union Cemetery. An endless hill; we left Margaret at the top, with little Peggy in her wicker basket. We sailed down, down, down—I was stretched out on top of Don's large sturdy back, holding on. Sailing down.

He remarked with some surprise that I was really a good little sport.

How could he have known that it was the best day of my life, so far?

Strangely, perhaps, I do not remember the arrival of my mother, come to take me home, nor what must have been a somewhat strained family reunion. What I do remember is that the night she arrived one of my front teeth, baby teeth, came out—for me a wonderful, significant event. I thought I looked terrific; I looked like Uncle Don.

I spent the whole trip up to Madison giggling at my reflection in the dashboard, a reflection that distorted the oval shape of my head, making it round. I kept saying, "Look at my teeth! Don't I look like Uncle Don?"

At last my mother could not stand it, my coldhearted, unwelcoming silliness, and she cried out, "No! Of course you don't look like Don, you little fool. What's the matter with you, anyway?"

How could I have told her, even had I known, that I was in love?

9

One morning, out shopping for fish on Clement Street, in a Chinese market, I recognized an almost familiar sweater: crude wool, variegated colors. I then saw that it was Caroline Houston, in the sweater that she had worn to her parents' party, that crazy Sunday. She greeted me pleasantly enough, though without effusion, real or otherwise. I was a little surprised when she said, "I live just a block from here. Would you want to come by? I could make some tea."

I accepted, we both finished our fish transactions and together we walked a block down Clement Street.

Caroline's studio was a huge bare room, one flight up above a grocery store. At one end there was a wide mattress on the floor, covered with something bright, woven wool. And along the walls there were big woolen sculptures, almost obscured by giant ferns. At the other end of the room was a kitchen area, a table and a couple of chairs, small refrigerator, stove. A wall telephone.

We were sitting at her kitchen table, drinking fragrant and very hot tea, when she abruptly told me about her parents: they had just split up, she said.

"So dumb, the way she left" was how Caroline put it to me. "Sneaking out in the middle of the night, after one of their parties." Her face and her voice showed total exasperation; she had had it with crazy grown-ups, with her parents. Caroline, about twenty-two.

"Sneaked out in the middle of the night" did seem a strange way to end a marriage. I asked, "She left a note?"

"No, no note. Dad was really upset. Of course he saw her car was gone, but Jesus, she could have driven over a cliff. Or jumped off the bridge."

That was quite true, I thought, remembering Ruth's desperate face, her slightly crazy delivery. And I thought, Well, this will make things easier for Royce and Stacy, and I felt a little envious: how nice for lovers when people just move out of their way, and how infrequently that happens. And how unfair that it should happen to Stacy, already so gifted with beauty, and with money.

However, I next thought, maybe Stacy would not be entirely pleased? Maybe Royce was not quite rich enough to be acceptable as an unmarried man? Maybe he was only as rich as her former husband had been, which wouldn't do.

"Finally Dad called her office," Caroline went on, "and there she was. She's living there, on Pine Street. She told him that she'd never been happier in her life."

"Couldn't that be true?"

"Oh, sure, I guess. Actually I don't see why he's so shook up about it. He keeps going on and on about the terrible neighborhood. How she'll get beaten up, or shot, or something."

"Well, that can happen anywhere." And I told her about the woman on my street out walking her dog and her husband getting shot, my first week in San Francisco. Caroline seemed not to have read about it, and I gave her points, at least, for avoiding the local papers.

In fact, she couldn't seem to focus on anything other than her parents' splitting up, although their story obviously irritated and depressed her. To my account of the murdered man, his wife and the dog, she merely said, "Oh, wow," which I already knew was not the way she talked.

Then, "Let's leave this mess," she said, gesturing at the cups and saucers, the teapot. Not my idea of much of a mess, but Caroline was a tidy person; the whole room showed that she was.

We went down to the other end of the room, and we both sat—or, rather, sprawled—on the piles of pillows there, beneath the long windows, at that hour filled with strong western sunlight streaming in. In that illumination I saw for the first time that Caroline's brown hair was really a combination of yellows and golds, like her sweater. I told her how pretty I thought it was, her hair. "It's the liveliest brown I've ever seen," I said—which was true.

"Oh, it's just clean," she said. "I'm a clean-hair freak." But she was pleased. I think women of her age don't compliment each other much, or not on things like pretty hair; in their way they are much more serious than we were.

The telephone in the kitchen area rang just then, a long turned-down sound that Caroline seemed attuned to. She got up, excusing herself, and went back to that corner of the room.

During her monosyllabic but rather prolonged conversation, I looked around—having tendencies to snoopiness. However, Caroline was so orderly, everything put away, that there was not much to see. Therefore, the pair of earrings on top of her bookcase struck my attention for several reasons: most obviously, because they were duplicates of the ones ripped off from me; secondly, that seemed a funny place for them to be, as though Caroline had for some reason not known what to do with them; and third, I could not imagine her wearing them. With so much long hair, big earrings wouldn't work; they were not in her style at all.

And looking at those earrings made me nervous, perhaps foolishly; I next concentrated on her books. A sympathetic, if not distinguished library, it was at least eclectic: Jane Austen, Colette, some Dickens, too much Anaïs Nin; Forster's *Howards End*—somehow this last was the most unlikely inclusion; odd to see a copy of my old favorite book in young Caroline's library. Eldridge Cleaver, H. Rap Brown, Marcuse, Tolkien, Jung.

I looked up at the earrings again. Most likely she had got them at Magnin's, I decided; maybe a present from her father, Royce?

Or maybe Caroline had been the thief?

That thought, as irrational as it was unavoidable, flooded me with a sudden extreme embarrassment at having entertained it for even a second. And as soon as the thought had gone, I thought, How crazy, untrue, impossible. And then I forgave myself.

Coming back, Caroline said, "That was a friend of mine. He's a carpenter, in fact, and I said he could come over for a minute. You don't mind? If you're still looking for someone—"

Then she looked over at where the earrings lay, and she said, "Someone just gave me those. I really don't like them very much," and she blushed.

It was Whitey who ripped off, burglarized my house. And he gave the earrings to Caroline. Those two sentences raced through my mind with the steel-cold ring of truth, and I too blushed.

However, a minute later I decided that he of course would not have told Caroline where they came from. If she knew or guessed that he had stolen them, she would certainly not know from where, or whom. And so I was able to look up and face Caroline, who had begun to talk about her parents—again.

She said, "You know, in her crazy way I think my mom is still crazy about my father."

She had spoken so unhappily; for that and every other reason I decided against mentioning Stacy, and offered, instead: "But even if that's true, couldn't they possibly be better off not together?"

Caroline looked sadder yet. "I just don't think so. I don't know; I'm sure it's all going to get a lot worse."

She was very convincing, and certainly her unhappiness was real. From some comforting impulse I asked her, "Have you thought about moving away somewhere? Mightn't it be easier for you if you weren't around all this?"

This seemed to strike Caroline as quite an aberrant suggestion. "But where would I go?" she asked. "I've been to New York a couple of times, and I really hated it there."

Later I came to understand that this was a very San Franciscan attitude. Where else *could* you live? was the usual position. As a stance I found it quite hard to imagine, always wanting to stay in the place where you were born, and where you had grown up. I liked Madison, my native place, very much indeed; I still feel nostalgic, sometimes, about the lakes, the pink twilight winter vistas of snow in the hills that surround the town. But that nostalgia is rather for my adolescence, which was spent among those scenes. Unlike most people I know, I loved the years from about thirteen to twenty, except for time out at St. Margaret's; I disliked my earliest childhood years, and those that began with my marriage but I have wonderful memories of dances and necking in steamy parked cars. I loved all that. But I couldn't wait to get away from Madison; I was always led on by visions of New York or London, Paris. And I sensed that Caroline would not even be tempted by those places. They were too far from San Francisco.

In fact, their mania for their city could be seen as a sort

of trap for San Franciscans; they are caught and bound in civic affection. And as I think of this, there comes to mind a picture that undoubtedly originates in Forties newsreels: people are leaving a besieged or ruined city; they walk in groups along a highway, carrying their pitiful possessions. In the case of a bombed-out San Francisco, this march would take place across one or both of the bridges, or down a superhighway to the Peninsula, the south. And with these visions came my notion that the city was a trap, as beautiful as it was confining.

Someone knocked at the door. Caroline went to open it, and she came back with what I can only describe as the loveliest young man I had ever seen. A beautiful brown boy, at first he looked; on second glance, he was a little older, maybe thirty. Blackish soft curly hair, long-lashed dark eyes, a curving mouth. Tall and graceful, lithe, with brown-gold skin. God knows what ethnic mix produced him: Tony Brown. Caroline introduced him, and he shook my hand formally. His hands were smaller than mine, but hard and strong.

Tony Brown was not only beautiful, but he was nice; his niceness and gentleness were instantly clear. And if I have made him sound effeminate, I didn't mean to. He was just beautiful to look at, and clearly of a gentle disposition. I was as drawn to him in a positive, human way—okay, also attracted—as I was turned off by Whitey.

He had brought some drawings of an interior, a living room. Caroline later told me that he had drawn them himself; they were beautifully, delicately done.

He spread them out on the floor, and we all peered down as Tony pointed to a fireplace and to the broad blank hood above it, surrounded by an intricate splaying of beams.

He said, "That's all brass, the whole hood. Lord, the money they're throwing into this place. But I thought maybe something of yours could go right there, Caroline. If you felt like doing it."

Tony's voice was soft, his accent lilting and vaguely "foreign"; Jamaican? Balinese? His tone, as he spoke to Caroline, was tentative, somewhat shy.

She said, "I don't know, it's a little too rich for my blood. I just can't see anything of mine hung up there. And all those fucking beams. It's really pretentious as hell."

"Well, it's totally up to you," Tony told her. "I just said I'd ask you. And they're really loaded." This last was a hesitant afterthought.

"So I see. And I could use the dough." She sighed. "Well, I'll see."

Tony Brown, the tasteful, scrupulous carpenter. I was not quite so rash as to hire him on sight, but I almost did.

He was saying to Caroline, "And later we could check out what's happening at the Boarding House, if you felt like it."

She seemed to consider, and then she said, "I'll think about it. I'll call you later on."

He smiled, accepting this answer as though used to it. Caroline did not quite smile back.

Whereas to me that small exchange had been amazing. Always with men I had said such an emphatic "Yes," or "No." Never a cool "I'll think about it." And certainly never "I'll call you." That was what *they* said.

I also thought that it was time for me to go, but just then beautiful Tony Brown got up and said that he had to go and meet someone, something about a job. We shook hands again, as formally as before; we said how nice to have met. Tony didn't shake hands with Caroline, nor for that matter did they kiss goodbye. They just vaguely waved at each other, and Tony walked across the room and out the door.

I asked Caroline if he was really a good carpenter.

"Oh, he's really good," she said. "He and Whitey used to work together but they fell out. I think now they're not even speaking to each other. Well, I have to admit it, Whitey isn't the easiest person in the world to get along with," and she sighed, as she often seemed to do when talking about her family.

What she had said struck me as confirmation of my own judgment: a nice and beautiful boy who had fallen out with Whitey could not be all bad.

And in that way I found the carpenter for Agatha's house.

10

By mid-November of that year there had been no rain in northern California, nor snow up in the Sierras, two hundred miles away. A dangerous situation: potential drought, water shortages. Still, it was hard not to enjoy the balmy, golden weather, the vistas of sunlight out on the Bay, the clear skies, the dry yellow sycamore leaves that crackled in any light breeze and scudded along the gutters, reminding me of Paris, other falls. Reminding me of Jean-Paul, for whom I still pined.

Mainly, though, that fall I was absorbed in doing Agatha's house. I had indeed called Tony Brown, and together we had worked out a remodeling plan: a wide deck off the kitchen, with space for pots of flowers, maybe a couple of lemon trees, some herbs and a broad bench for sitting in the sun. And above that deck there was to be a narrower one, just off the largest bedroom, which would be Agatha's. The bedroom in which I was now more or less camped out.

Tony got right to work, and he was a steady joy to watch, and just to have around.

He really liked to work. He usually arrived a little early, around eight; he would be smiling, humming something, eager to get started. And his work was fast, deft and competent. All this in addition to his beauty: Tony was a prize.

I assumed that he and Caroline were lovers, although without too much reason for that assumption. Just that sometimes he would ask if he could use the phone, and then I would hear her name. Or sometimes, when I was with Caroline, she would mention him, although more or less in passing.

I spent considerable time scouting for furniture and fabrics, and walked a lot, admiring that most beautiful city. I had an occasional cup of tea with Caroline, out in her Clement Street studio, and an occasional dinner with Agatha, usually in some restaurant. In fact, I was finally living as I had often thought I should: alone, concentrating on work, getting exercise, seeing only a couple of friends. No "social" life, not much to drink and nothing that even resembled a love affair. And I was as content as I could ever remember being. Just sometimes a little frustrated, which I didn't really think about.

Then one afternoon Agatha called, and she asked if I was free that night: could I come over to her place for dinner? That was unusual in itself; Agatha does not have much of a feeling for food, and we had both enjoyed our mutual exploration of the city's cheap ethnic fare. And then she said something even more unusual: tight-voiced, with a tight, small laugh, she said, "I seem to have this problem."

Well, a problem that could not be discussed in a public restaurant. Was Agatha finally in love with someone? Could she be pregnant? A variety of such fantasies went through my mind as I said yes, I'd love to come, I'd be there around six-thirty.

Curiosity, I guess, as well as my compulsive punctuality, made me get there somewhat early; it was only six-fifteen when I found a parking space on Polk Street, near her corner. Not wanting to fluster a nervous cook, and one with a problem on her mind, I decided to walk a few blocks.

Polk Street at that time was, and maybe still is, a mecca for hard-core, out-front leather gays. Lots of bared chests, and earrings, some makeup, dyed hair, extremely tight pants and high-heeled shoes. As I walked along, among those "gay" guys, I felt more and more uncomfortable, and at the same time a little guilty over my discomfort.

I was glad when it was time to go to Agatha's.

Whenever I went to her house, the flatness of Agatha's taste made me wonder why she would ever want a decorator, even me, her old friend. Her apartment was like a disguise, and maybe that is just what she was doing, hiding herself there among all that blond Danish modern—what was not Danish was upholstered in corduroy. I had plainly told her that all of it would have to go, which made her very unhappy until she thought of a needy place to give it to.

That night the rooms looked a little messier than usual, but there was a pretty bowl of spring flowers on the coffee table—out of character for Agatha to buy, her taste running more to daisies.

And she looked even more flustered than usual.

Again I thought, Ah, she's having an affair with someone, and that's what I'm here to hear about. The old expert on troubles of the heart.

She said, "I'm sorry I'm so disorganized. Someone came by for a drink, and stayed longer than I'd planned." She blushed, confirming my suspicions.

First we talked, as in these days we often did, about how her house was coming along. I said how pleased I was with the work of Tony Brown, how displeased with delays in fabric shipments, upholstery workshops.

I said that I'd seen Caroline, and that things sounded bad between her parents: separated, no one happy. At that, Agatha's face assumed a closed look which over the years I had learned to read: it meant that she had seen one or the other of the Houstons; one of them would have come into her office, probably, to talk to her. Ruth, most likely.

Agatha gave me a glass of wine, and we moved into the kitchen. By then I was quite hungry, looking forward to food and wine, as well as to hearing about her love affair.

Pot roast, and baked potatoes.

"I'm afraid I've overdone it," she apologized as we sat down at her blond maple table.

"Agatha, you can't overdo pot roast, it's really good." And it was, accidentally, one of her best efforts. I was enjoying my food, along with the anticipation of interesting confidences. But why was she so long in getting to it?

At last she repeated the words that she had said before: "Well, I seem to have this problem," and she smiled, in her old wry way.

"Oh?"

"Yes. It's sort of crazy." She paused, it seemed for a long time, while I waited. "It appears," she said at last, "that some woman in Washington is contesting the General's will. They were—I guess 'intimate' is the word, and she feels left out. She says that he made 'certain promises.'"

"Jesus Christ" was all I could say, out of a complex of reactions: disappointment, since talking about the General with Agatha always made me uncomfortable; we both knew that he was an ass, or worse, but that was impossible to say, he being her father. Also I felt genuine surprise; the General had been most adept at keeping out of scandals, not always an easy thing for a hyperactive playboy in a town like Washington.

And then I had another thought. "It could be sort of interesting," I said, rather heedlessly. "It might bring out how he came by all that money. Someone like Jack Anderson will wonder."

"I thought of that," said Agatha unhappily. "It could be a lot more embarrassing than interesting. And would it really do the world a lot of good to find out that he bribed the right Koreans, or took bribes from Iranians? Well, I guess it could."

I suddenly felt awkward, apologetic, and I saw something that I had not quite known before: I saw that I cared more about Agatha's possible discomfort than disclosures of national moment. I thought of Forster's remark about preferring to betray his country rather than a friend, and I wondered, How would Jean-Paul feel about that, such a highly personal morality?

"I really hate all this." Agatha spoke with unusual vehemence, forthrightness. "I think that woman really should get some money, if he promised it to her. I don't need as much as I have, God knows. But my lawyer says I absolutely must not get in touch with her. We have to wait. In fact he seems to take a very dark view of her character. But I don't care about her character."

"What a mess." It really was, and as I thought about it, it seemed worse and worse. I understood belatedly how nice it had been with the General just peacefully dead, leaving Agatha rich and me usefully occupied. Agatha no longer embarrassed by his love affairs and his Grecian Formula hair, nor enraged by his politics.

Agatha said, "It certainly is a mess. Betty Smith is the lady's name. You see? I couldn't get in touch with her if I wanted to." And then she said precisely what I had just thought, a thing that happened fairly often with us, no doubt a function of our having been friends for so long. She said, "It was so nice with the General just peacefully dead, wasn't it."

11

Such a surprise: the money from my robbery turned out to be a much larger settlement than I could have imagined; my secret certainty is that somehow a mistake in my favor was made. Agatha would have investigated; I did not, but deposited and spent the money as fast as I could. I had a wonderful time replacing my wardrobe.

That year the clothes were what advertising copy terms "classics"; as I see it, my height makes classics necessary, and so I bought blazers and skirts and pants, silk shirts—the classiest classics I could find, and I had never, really, been so well turned out.

Strange, if it was really Whitey whom I had to thank for all that finery.

Out of old habits of thought—or, rather, of feeling—for a while it seemed too bad, and sad, that no one (that is to say, no man, no lover) was around to appreciate my fashionable look, but then I thought, No, that's ridiculous. I'm dressing for myself.

One Sunday—I'm afraid partly out of an impulse to get dressed up—I went to church with Agatha. It was a small, very pretty church, on Union Street. And the funny thing is, I really enjoyed it, sitting there in the stained-glass filtered light, among all those nice-seeming serious people, listening to the hymns and prayers, the collects and lessons, thanksgivings. Or, "enjoyed" is not quite right: actually I was deeply moved. I had known all those words all my life, and to me they were entirely beautiful. At the same time, however, I experienced a kind of guilt in my pleasure; after all, I didn't really believe all that, not in the way that Agatha did. It was okay for her to enjoy going to church; for her it would be an experience of quite another order.

Then I had a curious but apposite memory: I was with Jacob, on the porch of one of those Atlantic coast hotels that he favored in midwinter—this was in Ocean City, Maryland, the same hotel in which he later turned me on to dope. We sat in high Victorian wicker chairs, overlooking the boardwalk, rocking, talking about what we had been reading, what novels, what poetry. And I confessed to Jacob that while I very much enjoyed reading poetry, and had read a fair amount, I often guiltily felt that I was not entirely grasping it.

And Jacob said, "But guilty, how perfectly ridiculous. If you enjoy it—fine. Any poet would be delighted. I, for example, often read Neruda in Spanish, of which I know only a very few words." Later he confessed that he liked to get really stoned and read Sappho in Greek, which he did not know either.

If I sound elegiac speaking of Jake, it is because he died a short time after that. A sordid heroin O.D., so unnecessary, so terrible. Alone, in a Howard Johnson motel, near Portland, Maine.

But remembering Jacob made me decide that it was okay for me to enjoy an Episcopal service, probably—and how terrifically funny he would have thought that was. "You gentiles are all alike, *au fond*," he might have said.

After church Agatha and I went out to lunch, on Union Street. We chose one of those ferny places with an open patio that are awful at night, crowded body shops, but perfectly pleasant for a Sunday lunch. We ordered white wine and crab, and we talked about what a pretty day it was. Sunny November, California basking in the drought.

Out of the blue, then, Agatha said, "There seems to be a Chilean connection."

"Whatever are you talking about?" Such a strange remark; at first I had thought she must mean the wine.

"The General seems to have spent most of the last few years with some very rich Chileans, and after Allende was killed he and 'Betty Smith' spent a lot of time down there, in Santiago."

"Jesus."

"I told you it would get worse and worse."

"Yes."

"In fact one of his last letters to me was his usual line of vituperation—come to think of it, maybe stronger than usual. He'd seen my name on some petition, something supporting Allende."

"What a total bastard." This slipped out; I do know that it's dangerous to bad-mouth other people's families, even hated ones, like possibly murderous right-wing generals.

But Agatha agreed. "Yes, it's hard to think of a redeeming feature," she said, and then, with a tiny laugh, "The General was always a strain on my notions of Christian charity."

I laughed too, but I felt a sort of chill: suppose it did

come out that the General had been involved in the murder of Allende? I found it easy to believe that in some very high-level financial way he had, and for all I knew in Vietnamese-Korean high-level bribes and scandals prior to that as well. I found it harder, though, to imagine the ramifications that would follow the public disclosure of such activity on the part of an American general, a West Point graduate, class of '32. Except for the embarrassment to Agatha, it would be quite wonderful, really. In much the same way that Watergate was wonderful, those hearings so deeply gratifying to watch, so assuaging, for a time, to one's most punitive instincts.

The waiter arrived with our crab—a welcome diversion. I could not exactly tell Agatha that I was looking forward to the posthumous disgrace of her father.

At a table across from ours was a handsome young Californian couple, athletic-looking, both very blond. I watched their play of smiles, touching hands, and heard them laugh. They were obviously just out of a late Sunday morning happy bedtime, and mean-spiritedly I thought, How do you two get to be so happy? I knew this to be absolutely unfair, not to mention uncharitable; it was perfectly possible that they were most deserving of happiness—were kind and talented, generous people, as well as handsome and happy. But I doubted it.

Partly to break that ugly mood, I said to Agatha, "Why don't we do something really Californian this afternoon? It's so beautiful. Maybe we could drive up to Mount Tamalpais. Hike about."

Agatha blushed before she answered. "I'm sorry, but I can't. I'm meeting Royce."

"Oh."

"Well, yes."

I'm afraid I sat there staring at her for a while, taking it in, thinking: Agatha and Royce.

Agatha and Royce.

12

The metamorphosis of Agatha: overnight, it seemed, from being a silent, withholding listener, once she had started she talked endlessly about Royce. His fascination for her was apparently interminable, every aspect of his history, his character. Of course I did not feel quite that way about him, but I tried to summon what interest I could; over the weeks that followed our revelatory Sunday lunch, I listened and took in a great deal about Royce.

His parents had come out from the Oklahoma dust bowl, in the early Thirties. But their luck was always just slightly better than that of those around them.

To begin with, their skills were fortunate. Josiah Houston, Royce's father, may have been a mechanical genius; in any case he was incredibly skillful with cars; he could diagnose and usually cure any of their ailments. Thus the Houstons' Ford kept running faithfully when other cars just died and were abandoned to rust and corrosion in some hot dry California ditch, a host to weeds. Deborah Houston sewed; she was a perfectionist, fanatical over perfect seams and finishings; when things were at their worst, around 1932, the year Royce was born, she would stay up most of the night turning collars and cuffs, so that worn-out shirts were good for another six months, and well worth the twenty-five cents she charged. Sometimes Josiah would fix someone else's car, and that gave him an extra buck or two. And so they did not quite starve on the starvation migrant-worker wages they were paid for picking fruit and vegetables, in the rich San Joaquin Valley, near Stockton and Modesto.

But maybe the Houstons' most important reason for luck was that they were both such large and strong, exceptionally handsome people. Josiah's height, and his thick white-blond hair (like Royce's), his blond moustache must have engendered some respect, as did Deborah's strict tall dark beauty. It is very possible that even the growers were nicer to them because they looked so good, not beaten down and haggard, gaunt, like so many of those migrants. And the Houstons were churchgoers, Presbyterians; they stayed away from the Communist agitators, union organizers, Eastern Jews.

By the time Royce was three or four—always the tallest, handsomest child around—his father, Josiah, owned a small farm in the delta, near the slews; ten years later, when Royce was in junior high, his father owned and ran the Ford agency in Manteca.

Royce as an adolescent was a natural athlete, terrific at every sport: captain of the football team, a baseball star, champion swimmer, all that. He even learned to ski, in the nearby Sierra foothills—then a crude, homespun sport. Royce loved skiing, the dizzying downhill rush, like flying, in the dazzling clean white snow.

He was curiously shy with girls—the truth was, he was a little afraid of them. He believed that girls were supposed to stop whatever you were doing to them; chastity was up to girls. But sometimes, maybe at a houseboat party on the river, among the thick dark sheltering rushes on a hot summer night, he would be feeling a breast, or groping with his hand up the bottom of a two-piece bathing suit, and the girl would just breathe harder, maybe moan, so that he had to be the one to stop, and later relieve himself in the shower. Fortunately, he had never felt much guilt about that practice; his parents never mentioned it. How could they? What words would they use? And the coach had delicately hinted that it was okay, a normal outlet, relaxing.

At some time during those adolescent years of Royce's, his mother, Deborah, in a strange way began to not make sense. Her speech seemed foggy, confused, and she took a lot of naps, at odd times. She died when Royce was seventeen, and then they found out what had been the matter: sherry bottles, hidden all over her bedroom, the room that for years she had not shared with Josiah. An alcoholic: they could hardly believe it, Josiah and Royce. Sober, Presbyterian Deborah, with her strong beliefs in work, in dedication to God, in Predestination and Original Sin.

When Royce was eighteen, and working in his father's Ford showroom, but dreaming, always, of San Francisco, he met a girl who not only did not push away his hands; she reached for him, and on her insistence they "went all the way." Later she said that she was in love with him. Ruth Estiz: her people were Basques, from up near the Nevada line. She had come down to Manteca to learn to be a secretary.

Royce loved her too, and all the sex they had was wonderful; he had not been sure a girl would like it too. They were married one Christmas, in the Presbyterian church that Deborah used to attend, although by now Josiah had left that church for something called the New Church of Christ, a group with strong feelings about Communists, of whom Josiah had had a bellyful during the Thirties.

In the spring Ruth and Royce moved to San Francisco,

and although Ruth was pregnant by then she got a good job as a legal secretary.

Discouraged by the showrooms on Van Ness Avenue, Royce got a job in a new foreign-car place, in Mill Valley, and that is where they lived, a small house in a new subdivision there, surrounded by magnificent old trees, oaks and pines, eucalyptus, redwood, looking up to Mount Tamalpais. It was 1953.

Caroline was born the following September, and Royce junior—Whitey—ten months after that, a miscalculation that for a while was pretty hard on Ruth, two such young babies and not much money yet. But Royce adored those babies; he was always touching and kissing them. During the early evenings he played with them constantly, and during the weekends at home he sang to them; later he read books and threw balls with them. "Spoiled them" Ruth at some point began to say, which would set off a soon to be familiar argument over possible interpretations of Dr. Spock: what *was* spoiling, anyway?

By this time, Royce was out of the car business and into real estate, where in the late Fifties and early Sixties he began to make a great deal of money in Marin County. However, it seemed to him that Ruth was restless, discontent, and he encouraged her to go to law school, an old dream of hers. She studied hard and did extremely well, and after passing the bar she got a job with a small firm, and then a year later she opened her own office, in a Victorian house out on Pine Street.

Royce was rich and Ruth was very busy, and the kids were good-looking, happy-seeming adolescents, and everything should have been wonderful, the opposite of Royce's own somewhat pinched youth—he had begun to think that both his parents had been more than a little crazy—but it wasn't wonderful. Ruth became almost totally involved in various causes: civil rights, peace, eventually women; she was always at meetings and marches, writing letters, more meetings, and she and Whitey fought all the time, which made Caroline cry, made Royce wretched. Partly in reaction to all that trouble at home, he immersed himself in the rich social life of Marin County, lots of new friends in Ross and Kentfield, Belvedere. He distrusted the Sausalito–Mill Valley element; they looked like nuts to him.

Among the new friends was Stacy Page, at that time a very rich, just-divorced young woman—leery of ambitious bachelors, a perpetual flirt with most married men. Not unaware of how wonderful they looked together, both so tall and blond, she and Royce flirted a lot, for several years, at parties.

They flirted, until one morning Stacy called and invited Royce to lunch. During the drive over the hills from the Stinson Beach house, which they had just built, to Stacy's place in Belvedere, Royce was unaccountably nervous, although he told himself that there would be other people, including her maid and the Filipino houseboy. He had been to Stacy's huge high-up balconied house before; Stacy liked lunch parties, and the hastiness of this particular invitation probably just meant that someone else couldn't come, some other man. After all, by now they were almost old friends, he and Stacy Page.

Stacy met him at the door, visibly alone, in gray linen pajamas; she led him into the living room, and he observed that she was quieter than usual, smiling rather than saying anything. She led him toward several bottles of chilled white Burgundy, a fish salad, cheese and coffee. And then she led him upstairs to her wide blue-flowered bed, with its view of Mount Tamalpais and the Bay, lots of sky, clouds, birds.

Even that first hyper-excited time there were certain problems about love with Stacy. For one thing, she was an awfully big girl; even big Royce felt lost within her. (Delicate Agatha put this to me as delicately as she could, simply saying, "Well, Stacy is awfully *big*. I mean, she made Royce feel—") For another, although she must have been fairly experienced by then, she performed certain acts as though she had heard about them and always meant to try them out sometime; her performance was a little academic. True sensuality, real driving lust, did not seem to be what motivated Stacy.

Whereas Ruth was and continued to be a deeply sensual woman. Madly "in love" with Stacy, Royce still had a better time in bed with Ruth. Very strange; he could not figure that one out. Even, sometimes, he had a curious, unnerving sense that Stacy was using him in a sexual way. All those orgasms were good for her skin, kept her blood pressure low, something like that.

But they kept it up, he and Stacy, for quite a long time, well past the usual ten months of an intense illicit love affair. (This was Agatha's generalization, not necessarily mine.) They kept up both the party flirtations and the twice-a-week afternoons of screwing: one afternoon a week at Stacy's, on the help's day off; another at some carefully chosen motel. Stacy's favorite was the Flamingo, in Santa Rosa. "God, it's so *tacky*, it's *perfect*," she would cry out. Occasionally they would also take a swim in a motel pool.

Ruth moved out on a Wednesday night, and the next day, Thursday, being the help's day off at Stacy's, Royce was supposed to go over there for lunch.

A great mistake.

Having been told the news, over the ritual glass of wine, which they sometimes enlivened with coke, Stacy said, "Well,

I can see how you'd be a little surprised, but I honestly can't see why you're sounding so *gloomy* about it."

Gloomy: Stacy's most pejorative word; she was a positive thinker, basically.

Accused, Royce floundered. "I don't either," he admitted. "I guess I'm in some sort of shock."

Stacy that day was wearing a blue silk shirt, white pants. No bra. No shoes. Her small breasts and even her feet were very beautiful; Royce was often stimulated by the sight of those perfect toenails, polished, pink. But not today. In fact today he felt terrible.

Stacy continued, with a slight elevation of her lovely dimpled chin. "And I'm not exactly the ideal person for you to come to for sympathy in this case," she rather reasonably said. "Just think, Royce—*God*—now we can go out."

"Going out" with Stacy, Royce suddenly understood, was what in the entire world he least of all wanted to do. He did not even want to consider the possibility for some future occasion. He wanted to stay at home, and in his own way to mourn for Ruth, whom he had already begun to idealize, like a person who has died.

Or he would like to get drunk somewhere, and Stacy, like most highly self-conscious beauties, drank very little.

He managed to make love to her that afternoon, but only once, instead of their usual twice, or sometimes thrice. And then Royce went home and got drunk. Later Whitey came in, and the two of them really tied one on, as they put it to each other the following morning. They were both excessively hung over.

Royce remained extremely disturbed: Ruth refused to come home; she almost refused to speak to him. On some impulse Royce called Agatha and told her how upset he was. Maybe he could come over and talk to her?

Seated across from Agatha, the familiar family friend, in her funny, Danish-dowdy apartment, Royce tried to tell her how he felt; an essentially nonverbal person, he tried out phrases on her. Grown apart; conflicting interests; should have made more of an effort; not communicating. He said all those things, but none of them quite seemed to fit. He stopped trying, and just said that he felt sad. Miserable, in fact.

Agatha listened, as she does, and the more he talked the more he became aware of the quality of her listening, of her small sad mouth. What he really wanted, he suddenly thought, was just to take her out to dinner, to a nice quiet place. To be nice to Agatha.

13

Of course I thought, and thought and thought, about that long conversation with Agatha, which was by far the most intimate of our long association. And since I was really much more interested in her than I was in Royce—to say the least, what struck and interested me most were the revelations of her character.

Her compassionate concern for Royce I would have taken for granted, as I would have known that she would be touched by the fact of the family's being originally Okies; it was rather as I had felt about the working-class origins of Derek—and so much for reverse snobbery on both our parts.

What was new, and to me most surprising, was Agatha's clear familiarity with the mechanics and the pitfalls of illicit sexual affairs. Oh ho, so you've been there too, and quite extensively, is what I thought.

Another novelty was the unbridled malice with which Agatha spoke of Stacy; for Agatha, that had been a genuinely vicious description.

And again I thought, Oh well, then, we really have more in common than I had ever known.

*

In the midst of these and similar thoughts, plus a few constructive musings about Agatha's house, one morning I went out to the mailbox, not hoping for much, and there was a thick envelope from Paris. From Ellie Osborne. A news photo, and a long letter, which said, in part, "No, I have never met your friend Jean-Paul, but I have read about him a good deal in the press. You'd think a handsome man like that would get himself to a better barber, wouldn't you?"

The words brought back the nasal arrogance of Ellie's voice, the loud echoes of inherited money.

But I gave almost no thought to Ellie that morning, for there was Jean-Paul, staring out at me from a blurred black-and-white photograph. My hands were trembling, and my heart jumped around.

Ellie was right about the haircut, at least; it was much too short, shaved above the ears, giving him somehow a Middle Eastern look, or maybe Yugoslavian.

But his face.

What had been soft and smooth and boyish had hardened; at fifty, or whatever Jean-Paul would be by now, he was leaner, more taut than he had been at thirty. One thing I thought of was how totally wrong Derek had been, in all respects: Jean-Paul had got thin, not fat. And I would have known him anywhere.

He had a deeply lined high forehead, deep furrows down both cheeks, and still that dark indentation at the bottom of his chin. An anguished, perhaps an angry face. Silly Ellie had cut off the explanatory caption; the picture could have been taken at a political rally somewhere, or in the midst of a strike.

I was terribly, hopelessly moved by that photograph.

It was like falling in love with Jean-Paul for a second time, or maybe with a new, even stronger, even more exceptional Jean-Paul. And since I too, the person in love, was surely older and wiser and in most ways stronger now, the emotion was intensified.

When I was able to think clearly, or almost clearly, I began to run through various alternatives: I could write to him, or even telephone. After all, I never had, but people did call Paris—Derek was always making such far-off phonings. But I could not work out what to say. And there was always the slight but horrifying possibility that he would not remember me. I used to believe, in a very simplistic way, that one's own feelings about a person are an accurate indication of how that person feels about you, which is of course ridiculous. I think that for a couple of men, at least, whom I did not much care about, I have been a major love; and it could plausibly be that way in reverse for me and Jean-Paul. There I was, twenty years later, pining away, and he could wonder at the sound or the sight of my name: Daphne *who?*

The following week Ellie sent me another picture of Jean-Paul, this one clipped from some French newsmagazine.

The second picture was entirely different from the first, almost not recognizable as the same person. The hair was still short, but tidily, even smartly so, just a trim neat cut. And he was wearing a nice tweed coat—in the first picture his clothes had been as ill-fitting as his hair. A striped tie.

And he was smiling—a pleased, very interested and very sensual smile. Perhaps the photographer was a woman who attracted him? It was somehow an intimate picture, suggesting that possibility.

And I did not know which Jean-Paul was the more forbidding, the impassioned political leader, or the sophisticated, elegantly turned out man.

I had of course assumed love affairs for Jean-Paul, over the years. But I guess I had imagined that he would not have put in too much time in that way, being so busy. Unlike me. But in that picture it looked as though he had put in a lot of time, a lot of love affairs.

I could not work out an approach to him, nor what to say once I had thought of one.

14

One morning Tony Brown came in considerably later than usual, at almost nine. He looked terrible, as though ashes had been rubbed into his beautiful warm brown skin. When he opened the door, I was sitting in the kitchen eating breakfast. I thought he must be sick, but I didn't like to ask. Besides, we hardly ever had conversations beyond what was necessary in the way of directions from me, and his explanations about what he was doing, and where and when. Or when I praised his work. I felt much affection for Tony, of a restfully unconversational sort; it had seemed to me that much too much of my life had been taken up in conversation, not all of it constructive, or even always fun.

However, when Tony glanced down at my eggs and looked even more ashen, I knew absolutely what was wrong: the poor kid had a horrible hangover. I said, "Tony, for God's sake, sit down. I can't stand to see you looking like that."

He sat, with a grimace, and I went to fetch him a dose of Fernet Branca, with a water chaser, and then for good measure a bunch of Brewer's Yeast tablets.

He got all that down, with some effort, and he said, "You're right, I don't feel too good today. Me and Whitey, we ran into each other over on Potrero, and we decided to quit fighting each other. After all, we was buddies, over there. Then we went out to do some drinking, kind of to celebrate, and that man can really pour it down."

"Was Caroline along?" Instantly I wondered why I had asked that, and I very much hoped that it had not been out of curiosity about the sexual life of Tony Brown.

"No, I don't think she and him are getting along any too good these days."

That surprised me; I guess I had taken for granted the intense brother-sister connection that I had observed, and I may have thought too that Caroline would be an influence in bringing Tony and Whitey back together. She would want them to be friends, I would have thought.

But then, not having had any, I don't have too much instinct for sibling relationships. And one of the bad aspects of the only-child condition is that we are extremely inept at fights: we think that any fight is final; most of us are devastated by quarrels. In my imagination brothers and sisters fight all the time, in a cheerful bear-cub way, and then they quickly get over it—cleansed, as it were. But maybe they don't.

I asked Tony if Caroline and Whitey had had a fight.

"No, nothing like that. They don't fight too much. Whitey just gets real mean when he drinks, and I think Caroline's pretty much had it with his shit." He stood up then, announcing, "So am I, really tired of that man. I'm not going to do any more drinking with him, not any more."

I could not help feeling a mean-spirited sort of pleasure at the idea of Whitey's being shunned by his former friend, and by his sister. But at the same time it was a little frightening, the thought of Whitey unleashed on the world, looking for trouble, and revenge.

"Anyway, he's talking about going up to Alaska, getting work on the pipeline," Tony said.

"That sounds like a good idea."

"His dad's dead against it, but I don't think that's going to stop Whitey for long."

I didn't think so either, and then I began to wonder what Agatha's connection with Whitey was like, how she felt about him. At this point I did not feel I could ask her, and I wondered if she would ever say.

Already Tony was looking much better, almost his old self, and I considered enviously the recuperative powers of youth—although he was probably not ten years younger than I was. And that morning, as always, I was struck by the extreme cleanliness of all his clothes, the bleached-out work shirts, and faded jeans, never ironed but always just washed. The combination of that soft pale blue cloth with his lovely brown skin was beautiful. And my appreciation of Tony did not arise from a generalized hard-upness, I am fairly sure. I think that under any circumstances I would have found him enchanting to look at, as lithe and graceful as a cat, with those luminous dark eyes and lovely thick dark lashes.

Besides, as well as liking to look at Tony I *liked* him, and I daily blessed my luck in having him around. Incredibly enough, he was about to complete the work in the kitchen ahead of schedule, and to start on the small upstairs deck.

Some sudden strong impulse made me say, that morning, what I had often thought: "Tony, I really don't know what I would have done without you."

Tony's smile came slowly to his face, and it usually involved a sidewise motion of his head. He went through that gesture now, completing a strong full grin.

Conversely, I have noticed that people with flashing smiles, of the now-you-see-it-now-you-don't variety, are generally quite mean, hostile people. Derek smiled like that; the expression came from nowhere, and as suddenly disappeared. A grin without an emotion.

Tony just said, "I'm real glad it's worked out," and the smile remained.

I looked out at the neatly railed deck, its redwood floor, and at the deep rows of kitchen shelves, all clear smooth new wood, and at the round kitchen table and the benches against the walls, and I said that I too was very glad.

Then Tony got to work and I headed out to Clement Street, to visit Caroline.

Generally she was an early riser, early to start to work; over the phone she had said to come over around ten—she would take a coffee break with me. But when I got there, exactly at ten, she was still eating breakfast. With a huge black man, whom she introduced as Thomas Baskerville. He had an exceptionally deep voice, its inflections Deep South. As we shook hands, I liked him right away; he seemed a serious person, a man of consequence.

Caroline was very fresh-faced, bright-eyed, in her old brown corduroy robe, her hair long and loose. She was clearly crazy about this Thomas, in a way that seemed out of character for her—cool Caroline. She kept touching him, reaching for his hand, stroking his back as she passed with honey and milk for our coffee.

Sensing Thomas's strong, evident attractiveness, I had a guilty pang for Tony, so much smaller, so lovely but less powerful a man. Did Tony know about Thomas? Had they maybe even met? Wondering about all that, wondering how this generation worked out such things, I wondered too just who it was that Thomas so strongly reminded me of—and then I realized that it was Royce, both of them huge and confident men, with even the same narrowly shaped eyes, although Royce's were so green, Thomas's very dark brown.

The notion of what either of them would make of such a suggested resemblance was enough to make me smile.

Caroline and Thomas had been talking, it seemed, about Whitey's proposed trip to Alaska, the pipeline plan that Tony had just mentioned to me. I gathered that Thomas and Whitey were or had been friends; it later turned out that they had been in Vietnam together, along with Tony.

"It might be the best thing for that man," said Thomas, in his deep, judicial voice—it occurred to me that if he sang he would sound like Paul Robeson, a thing I would not have said, with its somehow racist implications. "There's just not enough action in this town for Whitey Houston," Thomas said.

"Living alone with my father is really getting to him," said Caroline, to me. "They just drink all the time, sitting around out there."

Caroline, and possibly Whitey too, did not seem to know about Agatha's involvement with Royce, which I found mildly disturbing. Why didn't they? Why did Agatha, with Royce, have to be in a more or less illicit position? I resented it for her.

Caroline continued, about her family: "Whitey really dug all those parties out there," she said. "He thought it was going to be like that for good, a houseful of blond hair and classy clothes."

This was, in fact, an extremely astute observation on Whitey's character, and as sad as it was accurate. I remembered how happy and satisfied Whitey had looked at the Houston party Agatha and I went to, that long-past Sunday. He must have thought that all his father's new friends constituted a genuine arrival, a permanent condition of fun. An opulent, fashionable life was to be his compensation for the rotten war—like the gaudy, glittering Forties that followed the end of *that* war. I did not think that Whitey made these historical comparisons, though.

Thomas got up then and said he had to go. I should have left before him, of course, but there wasn't time. He was just suddenly gone.

Caroline came back from seeing him to the door and sat down across from me.

I would have liked to say something about Thomas, but what? *Wow, he's really terrific:* that sounded ridiculous, and besides, it would be presumptuous for me to make any comment at all. I had not been invited there for an inspection of Thomas.

My instinct about that must have been right, for Caroline said, "Just let me throw on a few clothes, and we can start in with some samples."

I remembered then what I had come to Caroline's about: my present to Agatha. Caroline was to make a large wool sculpture, which I thought would be wonderful for Agatha's bedroom.

In a few minutes Caroline reappeared from the bathroom in jeans and a sweater. She stood for a while in front of the open shelves on which she kept her piles of wool; from time to time she would reach in for something, consider it, either put it back or drop it into the growing pile at her feet.

At last she bent and picked up all the samples from the floor and brought them over to me. And I saw that she had worked out a spectrum, gray-blues to gray, to blue, to black. She was going to make something beautiful, a perfect present for Agatha.

15

One afternoon, rather late, the telephone rang, and there on the other end was Derek, but Derek without the hollow sound in the background that indicates a long-distance call. It was Derek in San Francisco.

"Well, my girl, since I've come out all this way, you must surely allow me the pleasure of taking you out to dinner."

I was not busy that night, although of course I could perfectly well have said I was. But curiosity and possibly a habit of acquiescence to Derek prevailed, and I agreed that yes, we would have dinner. I did not suggest that he should come to my house for a drink, however; he was not to call for me—I would meet him in the bar of his Nob Hill hotel.

"But, my dear, this place has half a dozen bars," he argued, and that was true enough, since he was staying at the Mark Hopkins.

We settled on the Top, the famous Top of the Mark, where so far I had never been: it would never have occurred to Agatha to take me there, nor me to suggest it. My considerable fear of heights would have been one deterrent, along with the tourist reputation of the place.

And then we began, as we had often done before, to argue about where to go for dinner, since presumably a reservation must be made.

I mentioned a quiet, unpretentious French place that Agatha knew about, in North Beach. Excellent food. But Derek had been told that Trader Vic's was the place where really knowing San Franciscans went, the only place. He had also been given the quite erroneous impression that you had to have some sort of introduction, some pull in order to be admitted, and he in fact had just that necessary connection; he had a friend who could arrange it all.

Well. The Top of the Mark. Trader Vic's. Dressing, I reflected that for me this would be an entirely new version of San Francisco.

I have to admit I was glad that night of my good new wardrobe, my "designer" clothes, and at the same time I felt ashamed of needing them. And I thought about the essentially defensive nature of certain clothes, the armor that they provide for the insecure, which has nothing whatsoever to do with aesthetics, even with simple attractiveness. I have, or I had before my tasteful rip-off—for which I continue to believe that Whitey was responsible—an old yellow shirt in which I looked better than in anything else; there was something about that particular shade, and its softness was becoming. But even if I still had it, I couldn't—or wouldn't—wear an old cotton shirt to those Derek-chosen places. I needed my expensive uniform.

The express elevator to the Top went extremely fast, for a very long time, activating my acrophobia—and giving me time to think that this was a very poor choice for a meeting place. As soon as the door opened, I knew that I would hate it there: such huge views, from so terribly high up. Views of everything: other buildings, the Bay, both bridges, Marin County, Berkeley, Oakland—Christ, you could see everywhere.

But there was Derek at the bar, instantly seeing me, coming toward me—and I knew better than to remind him of my weak-minded fears; he would have enjoyed my discomfort, as he had before, when we flew together and he saw my tight grip on the seat divider.

"Well my dear, I must say that you look quite smashing" was his genial greeting, accompanied by a cheek-brushing friendly kiss. It was a good beginning, and I realized that, away from Derek, I tended always to concentrate on his evil qualities, his sadism and general insensitivity, his egotism, whereas I would forget his reliably good manners, his pleasant looks, even his considerable intelligence—all of which were apparent as we moved to a table and began to talk.

Thank God: no window table was available, and so I was able to situate myself with my back to the views. I planned to give Derek the flattering impression of total attention to him, rather than to our splendid surroundings, but of course he noticed and mentioned it right away.

"You're avoiding the views," he said, but then he made a very wrong guess. "Do you come here so often that it bores you?"

I said that actually I had not been there before, and I added that in fact I was not fond of such very *large* views.

"You probably don't like views because there's nothing you can do to them, is that it? Professional annoyance: how would you decorate a view?" He chortled with pleasure at this attempt.

It was another wrong guess, but in its way quite clever, I thought; in the case of many—maybe most—decorators he would have been right on, and I laughed appreciatively. I was thinking, Well, he's not such a really bad person; maybe I can stop excoriating myself for ever having loved him.

And then Derek began to talk about a book of short stories just out by a young man whom we both admired, and

I was reminded of another forgotten worthy trait of his: he always seemed to be waiting with something urgent to discuss with me, often of a flatteringly elevated nature, such as this most talented young man.

Actually, though, we liked this young writer for quite dissimilar reasons. Derek was drawn to him for his geographic range: he seemed to have lived everywhere, even to have fought in wars in several places, as Derek had. Whereas I liked the quality of his prose, and I liked too his affectionate view of the people he wrote about, especially the women. After so many years of male-stud novels, heroes fucking everything in sight and never *seeing* a woman, this young man's sexual tenderness was a vast relief. And for that I put up with his occasional wars and bloodiness. But he was still a very good choice as a conversational starter between Derek and me, reunited in this most unlikely place.

I had ordered, received and begun to drink a double vodka, which helped my view vertigo. After twenty minutes or so I was even able to look around, and to my great relief I found that some heavy fog had come in; it enveloped the tower we were in, so that only a few dim lights were visible. Above the din of the bar I could hear foghorns, their harsh and mourning bray.

Derek was saying, in what was for him a very low voice, "You see that red hair? Look, two tables over there. Looks unreal, doesn't it, that particular color? But it's genuine, I can tell. It's the shade of red that always goes with light blue eyes."

The old Derek, re-emerged.

He seemed very pleased with this odd piece of expertise, and so I let it go, but not without marking it down in my mind for possible future use.

Then he said that it was time to get on to Trader Vic's. Along with the entrée provided by his friend to that

exalted restaurant, Derek had evidently also been given in-
structions on how to walk there from the hotel. "Only a few
blocks," I was told as we started out.

We pushed along in the fog, windblown and cold, and
then I remembered Derek's deep aversion to cabs. I guess
everyone clutches somewhere, money-wise, but with Derek
I would often have happily paid the taxi fare myself, which he
would not allow either. He even had elaborately worked-out
theories about why, in many circumstances, it is better to rent
a car.

We turned left down a very steep street; normally I
would have been apprehensive, afraid of falling on my face
and breaking at least my neck, but tonight drink had made me
heedless. And, in what must have been record time, we made
it to the restaurant.

The entrance was probably deeply disappointing to
Derek—in most ways a man of taste. Not having his high expectations, I was merely surprised that the first room you entered, in a supposedly elegant restaurant, could possibly be so
tacky. It looked like a gift shop—well, it was a gift shop:
silly souvenir-type things for sale, the motif being South Seas.
There were even especially bottled vinegars, and cookbooks
by the owner of the place. And the group of people who
were already there, who had just made themselves known
to the maître d' and were being appreciatively made welcome,
did not look like a group with Derek's connections. They
seemed rather to be rich Texans, wearing pounds of chin-
chilla and vicuña, Gucci, thick eye makeup, diamonds and
gold. They reeked of oil.

"Hossein, this is absolutely the darlingest place!" I
heard one of the women cry out, and then I noticed Hossein,
the dark stranger in their midst, whose heavy brows gave him
a strong resemblance to his deposed Shah. Quite possibly it
was Hossein who was their host, and their connection.

Those people were taken off somewhere, and then Derek gave his name, and the name of his friend, and we were seated.

"You see? We're not in the same room with them," he observed triumphantly, but since neither of us was an expert on the status signs in that room, I thought that for all we knew "those people" got preferential treatment over us. Maybe "Trader Vic" was especially fond of Iranians and Texans—but I said none of this to Derek.

I was not, however, rewarded for restraint; instead Derek began to attack me for the tackiness of the place.

"Well my dear," he led off familiarly—we could have been married for years—"if this is what San Francisco considers grand, I do rather wonder at your choice of residence."

I countered weakly that I had never been there before, and realized with some surprise that I now felt defensive about San Francisco, although quite possibly that was because it was Derek who was doing the detracting. "And really, Derek," I went on, "do you often judge cities by their most pretentious restaurants?"

"Touché, my dear." Derek was generally a fair-minded person. "But it's not exactly Maxim's, is it now."

"I never said that San Francisco was Paris, or even *like* Paris."

"Well, at least you can't defend your morning newspaper."

"No, you're right there. I wouldn't think of it."

For a while we chattered amiably about the deficiencies of the *Chronicle;* that morning Derek had been struck, as most visitors are, as I had been a couple of months ago, by its extreme localness. I agreed, of course, and that small conversation almost restored us to friendship, or something near it.

We had more drinks, and then we ordered our dinner. Derek wanted something Oriental, as I guess he had been told to do. I ordered salmon, having become a great fan of West Coast fish.

Fresh drinks.

Over his new Scotch, Derek began to tell me again how marvelous I looked. He praised my clothes, and he said that it was wonderful for me to be so tall. He had not said this before—in fact I could remember quite a few complaints about my height—but now he went on at some length about the advantages, for a woman, in being tall. He couldn't stand an undersized woman, he told me. He spoke so venomously about short women that I knew he must be having an affair with one.

And then he asked me if I had ever thought of becoming a dancer. Well, that suggestion was ludicrous enough to make me laugh aloud. "Derek, for one thing, I have practically no sense of balance. You know that. I might as well take up tightrope walking."

During dinner, Derek made several remarks about women who couldn't cook—he knew that I could—and I made a note of that.

After dinner there was a belly-dance place that Derek had heard about. We had terrible drinks there, and above the dreadful music Derek shouted into my ear about what really awful people most dancers are.

Once you have noticed a persistent mannerism in another person, of course it becomes much more marked; the smallest hint of it looks like a caricature. I could hardly believe that Derek was going on and on with his old barely concealed jealousy ploy, but he was. He was worse than ever; or maybe his perception of my relative lack of response—not like the old days—was goading him on.

In any case, by that time we were really tired of each other, the difference between us being that I knew it, whereas

Derek did not. Leaving that place, I saw from his face that I was supposed to ask him back to my house for a nightcap; he may even have expected to spend the night. But I had been working on a sneaky plan of my own, and I suggested my "favorite" North Beach bar, where actually I had been only once; what I liked about it—or, rather, what conformed to my plan—was its layout: a long entrance hall, invisible to the main room, off which was a Ladies.

Leaving Derek in the big room, with his brandy, I wrote him this note from the Ladies: "Dear Derek, I'm sorry you're having trouble with your short red-haired blue-eyed non-cooking dancer. Better luck next time. I don't think we have much more to say to each other."

I sent the note in with a waiter.

I thought it was very funny, and I giggled drunkenly to myself all the way home in my Taxi. I knew that Derek would consider it beneath him to follow me home, or even to call, and I knew too that if he had come home with me there would have been an ugly scene.

In the morning, though, nothing seemed funny at all. I felt terrible, and the note to Derek appeared simply a childish gesture. For a long time I was too heavy-headed, too aching in all my limbs, to get out of bed, and so I just lay there, plagued and tormented by everything I had ever done that was wrong. From my Episcopalian years at St. Margaret's the General Confession came back to me, and ran dolorously through my head: "We have left undone those things that we ought to have done, and we have done those things that we ought not to have done." Well, that summed it up rather tidily, I thought. Maybe I could somehow rejoin the church, in a serious way, like Agatha? But probably not.

One of the things that I "ought" to have done, long ago,

was to run off with Jean-Paul. What a life that would have been! What a woefully missed opportunity it now seemed. That was my single chance for a significant, serious life, I thought—on that awful hung-over morning. Also, and I could handily blame Derek for this, I had not even tried to find Jean-Paul, the time we were in Paris.

The thought of Derek himself, that morning, was another source of self-laceration. How could I have had a lover, lost time and sleep over him, whom I didn't even like? When he was both mean and pompous, never mind about intelligent and handsome. It was very depressing, and it got worse as I considered an array of not-liked lovers—all of them shits, really, as I now saw it—with whom at one time or another I had been "madly in love." Only Jacob and Jean-Paul stood out, as liked and loved and tremendously admired. And Jake was dead, a savage junkie death, and Jean-Paul impossibly in Paris, busy being a leading Euro-Socialist.

At last my guilty ruminations began to seem ridiculous, even to me, and I forced myself up and out of bed, down to the kitchen for tomato juice, Fernet Branca and lots of vitamins. I was not up to eggs.

I was just dosing myself with those remedies when Tony came in. He took one look at me and then he did an amazing, if totally simple thing: he put his arms around me, he lightly kissed me and he said, "Oh, poor Daphne." I don't think he had ever said my name before.

It was a questioning, tentative kiss, however—an invitation rather than a gesture. Which I declined. Without a thought—this surprised me later on, when I did think about it—I said, "Ah, Tony, you're so nice, you make me feel much better," but in a clearly dismissing way.

He understood, of course, and smiled, and went off to work. I guessed that he felt a little relieved. He would have been agreeable to taking me to bed if I had wanted to, but I didn't think he really wanted that kind of complication either —nor, I had to face it, had he wanted me very much. I was the one with the sexual fantasies in his direction. He had just felt that he should make the offer of himself.

Which said a lot about Tony, and I began then to wonder how much of his charming posturing was accidental. Maybe he was the same sort of automatic flirt that Stacy, for example, was.

I wondered too about Tony's connection with Caroline; it seemed more and more likely that they were indeed "just friends."

God knows what Tony's true sexual nature was, I thought then—and how I wish that I had never happened to find out.

16

Like many people of my generation and my sort of education—an education involving good schools, good books and a lazy, haphazard sort of mind—my friends and I did a lot of emotional temperature-taking, so to speak. We were always very interested in how we were. Agatha alone was exempt from this preoccupation; I had decided finally that she was genuinely not interested in her own mental health—it was her spiritual condition that concerned her.

Other friends and I all used certain key phrases in regard to ourselves and others—phrases dull enough in themselves but for us significant. "In bad shape" meant terrible, nearly suicidal, probably; and so on upward, through various, intimately known gradations, until we arrived at "better," an ideal state. *I really think I'm better* indicated true happiness: not euphoria—we all knew the dangers inherent in that—but warm contentment, our goal. We were certain too that happiness meant some good balance of love and work, and probably some money.

Working on Agatha's house at that time, with no love affair going on, earning money, I really did feel better—there were my lecherous fantasies about Tony, about which I felt a little guilty, until I thought, Well, men have such fantasies about us all the time, or they say they do.

In fact I felt a lot better, until the night when Whitey

came over and I began to feel really terrible, and that evening could so perfectly easily not have happened at all.

But it did happen. Agatha was coming for dinner, and since I had to be out all afternoon, in search of some brass fittings for the bathroom, and, I hoped, some striped canvas for deck awnings, I made the dinner in the morning, a nice winey, garlicky stew, with lots of rosemary, which would be even better heated up for dinner.

However, when I got home late that afternoon, exhausted and unsuccessful, having found nothing that I liked in canvas or in brass, the phone was ringing as I opened the door. I ran to answer it—unfortunately forgetting the unlocked door— and it was Agatha, saying that she couldn't come. She was sorry; she had been trying to get me all afternoon, she said. Something had come up, with Royce.

I was furious and quite hurt, most irrationally so—although I did not say this to Agatha. I do react badly to changed plans about meals, something infantile to do with food, I guess. For another thing, I did think Agatha was being a little adolescent about her love affair; grown-up women don't break dates with each other because at that moment a man is more pressingly important to them, not any more.

I was so used to seeing Tony's battered VW in my driveway that I had not consciously registered seeing it just now, coming home, but in the throes of my disappointed anger with Agatha I remembered: the car was there, and so Tony was still here, in the house.

I ran upstairs and there he was, and I had to make an effort to restrain the joy I felt at the sight of him, tired dusty beautiful Tony, my reliable friend.

Attempting cool, I said, "Tony, I have a neat idea. I made some lamb stew this morning—why don't you stay and have it with me?"

I think I would have died, or cried, if Tony had said that

he was sorry, he had something else on for that night—as he very well could have said.

So maybe I was not so much better, after all?

But he smiled, in his lovely slow all-over way, and he said that that would be really nice. "Good coincidence," he said. "There's somewhere I haven't got to go either. I just found out."

I laughed, very pleased.

Tony asked if it would be okay if he took a shower. Of course.

He came out a little later, immaculate as usual; he had worn, that day, a wonderful red-polished shirt, as though he had known that he would be asked to stay to dinner.

I couldn't have had dinner with Tony, who looked so splendid, in anything ordinary, and so I put on a long yellow dress that I had bought with the insurance money—for heaven knows what purpose: perhaps this one.

And that is how it happened that about nine that night Tony and I were sitting at my dinner table, with candlelight and wine, in our intimate fancy clothes.

When Whitey walked in.

"What the fuck, you guys can't be bothered with locking your door?" That was how he greeted us.

And of course he was right: I had hurried in to answer the phone, not locked the door, maybe even left it slightly ajar.

His look accused us of not only leaving the door open but of some somehow ugly sexual complicity—as if all the fantasies I had ever had concerning Tony had been the actuality of our situation; in a sense, he was right about us—or at least about me. And certainly, I have later thought, if he had not showed up, the evening might have ended very differently. My asking Tony to stay to dinner was a little odd, as was the yellow dress—with Whitey, I felt guilty as charged.

Drunkenly he sat down across from us, staring enraged, his eyes going from one to the other of us. Occasionally, left-handed, he would reach up to scratch at his beard, so that the missing fingers were in blatant evidence.

God knows what was in his mind, but it almost didn't matter; he looked like a man out to kill whatever crossed his path, like someone in a war, out on patrol: Tony and I were random objects in his path. He began to mutter, incomprehensibly, under his breath, and I felt the swollen presence of murder in his eyes.

Crazily, or maybe because he understood Whitey in a way that I did not, Tony chose to behave as though everything were perfectly okay: a friend had dropped in to see two other friends, who happened to be having dinner together. Tony said, "You care for a glass of wine, man? I'm afraid we've done for the stew."

In the midst of my terror I was trying to work out just why Whitey hated me so much; the fact that I had not hired him to work on the house did not explain it. I thought it must be something visceral, or like an allergy.

Tony continued to make inane conversation, none of which Whitey answered. He just stared, eyes bulging with hatred, while I thought: The sharp knives are in the farthest kitchen drawer. Where do you stick a knife in a person if you just want to scare them, not to kill? Or maybe I should hit him with something heavy. How hard do you hit non-fatally? Impossible questions that certainly had never been anywhere near my mind before. But maybe those are things we all should know, along with first aid and how to dislodge things stuck in someone's throat.

Whitey was ignoring Tony's foolish, bland remarks—which, to my ears at least, had begun to sound grotesque. But then suddenly he turned fully on Tony—I could tell that he had forgotten I was there—and he shouted, "You're really at home here, aren't you, old asshole buddy—you fucking whore!"

An odd thing for a man to call another man, but Tony just looked at him, in an animal, patient way, in the echoing silence that followed Whitey's outburst.

Whitey was bigger and probably stronger than Tony, but he was drunk. If they really got into it, I would either knife or hit Whitey, I decided; fuck being fair.

Whitey kept on muttering and glaring murderously. Inside my yellow silk I felt sweat running down under my arms, under my breasts. It was hard to breathe. I didn't want to look at Whitey, but I couldn't not.

After what seemed like an hour but was probably ten or fifteen minutes, Tony stood up and said, "How about let's head out for a beer, Whitey, man?" And he looked at me. "You care to come along?"

I knew that he didn't mean for me to come, and of course I wouldn't have. I said no, barely getting out the sound.

Tony came around to where I was sitting and he gave me an unfamiliar pat on my shoulder, and then he went out the door.

Whitey lurched out after Tony, with a backward look of the purest rage, unfocused but in my general direction.

Once they were gone, I double-locked the door and checked all the street-level windows, and I checked the phone to see if it still worked. Whitey might even have cut the wires, I thought, as he came in. But it was okay.

The sweat on my body had turned cold; in fact I was shaking with cold, and pure terror.

Clearing the table and cleaning up the kitchen was difficult, but it took up a lot of time, until whatever was to happen next. I was sure that the night wasn't over yet.

Whitey could murder Tony, and then come back for me, I thought.

Or someone in a bar could kill them both, enraged by Whitey and assuming them to be one of a kind, in it together.

They could both be killed in an accident.

It was certainly clear to me that I was not *better*, after all: I was terrible; I was in bad shape.

But those tired old phrases made me smile, a little, for the first time in several hours.

I went upstairs with a book, and I stared at all the words, sometimes turning pages.

Around midnight the phone rang, and it was Tony; he was clearly drunk but he was also clearly alive. "Baby, you worry too much," he mumbled when I had expressed some tiny part of the fear that I had felt. "You take that Whitey too *serious*."

"Fuck you!" I shouted into the phone.

"Baby, I see you tomorrow."

I hung up, and then I began very weakly to cry, as much from exhaustion as from any nameable emotion.

17

Partly out of guilt, I am sure, for breaking our date, Agatha insisted on taking me out to dinner later that week; and she suggested a huge Chinese place out on Geary Boulevard. "It's so awful-looking that it's funny," she said. "But the food's terrific."

She was right all around. The décor consisted of a lot of red plush and green scrolls, and some horribly bright blue plumes in ornate vases. And the food was wonderful, delicately spiced and served with elegance, course by course, not all jumbled together as so often happens in lesser restaurants.

At first we sipped some wine and talked about what to order. Agatha was very nervous; I recognized the dry tightness in her voice, her slightly cracking laugh. We both knew that eventually she would tell me about Royce's emergency —she would have to, really—but in the meantime we both stalled.

The night of Whitey's visit was still very much in my mind. Tony and I were friends again, or whatever we were, but I felt scarred by having been so frightened; the terror that I had experienced, thinking about knives and blunt instruments, would not entirely dissipate. Some instinct made me not tell Agatha about it, though I wanted to, and would have welcomed any reassurance. But I felt that in a way it would have sounded like an accusation of Royce: like father like son, or something.

Groping about for something safe, a neutral topic, I came up with a book that a woman we both knew had written, and just published. Strangely enough, it was a novel about a prostitute; strange because Ethel, the writer, was as old as Agatha and I were—she too dated back to St. Margaret's—and she was a lot more square, or straight, whatever. The truth is, she was a very dumb and totally conventional woman. At St. Margaret's she had been famous both for dumbness and for tidiness, the oft-cited example being a term paper on which a Miss McGing, a wonderful dour wit among gloomier teachers, had given Ethel an A-plus over a D, the A-plus being for neatness and the D for content. Agatha, a messy person, had sometimes got just those grades in reverse. But in a way we both had rather liked Ethel: maybe we found her restful after heavy doses of brighter, more erratic friends.

The book was a "paperback original," which Agatha hadn't seen but I had; I'd read most of it standing up in Walgreen's at the paperback rack.

"Odd," Agatha said. "The last time I heard from her she was just going on about her house and children and husband, I think in that order."

I was mildly surprised at Agatha's having heard from Ethel at all; she had not been a particular friend of either of ours for years. But Agatha is the sort of person whom other people at stray moments think of, and then write to.

"The book is worse than you could believe," I told Agatha.

"Poor Ethel is really very dumb." From Agatha, this was an uncharacteristically harsh remark, except that sometimes she sounded like me. I suppose that I sound like her, on occasion, too.

"Such a mistake, dumb friends," I put in.

"The problem is," said Agatha, and I could feel her warming to the conversation, welcoming its abstraction as a relief from whatever was bothering her, "the trouble with dumb friends is that they don't recognize their function in your life. They don't see themselves as dumb friends."

I laughed. "No, and then they do something presumptuous like having an opinion about a book, or writing one, for God's sake."

This was the sort of talk we both liked: not quite personal and highly speculative. Amusing, or so we thought.

Agatha kept it up with more energy than usual, and I guessed that she was very anxious to postpone whatever was on her mind. "Of course, the fact of being your friends makes them think that they couldn't be really stupid," she said. "Daphne wouldn't have a stupid friend, they think."

"Oh, you're absolutely right, and I won't have any more dumb friends; they're just not worth it," I told her.

The conversation seemed to languish then, and I tried to push it along; I didn't much want to go on to anything else either. "But have you noticed how they're all absolutely marvelous housekeepers?" I asked, just having been struck, from somewhere, by that fact. "Ethel isn't the only dumb immaculate." And it seemed to be true: Ethel's Scarsdale house was always surgically clean—who would have known she was entertaining prostitute fantasies? All the dumb friends we could think of that night were also terrifically neat. We thought of some bright people who were also very tidy; Caroline was the first who came to my mind—but in general that was harder.

Some of our food came, and we talked about how good it was.

Then, abruptly, Agatha said, "I'm really worried about this Betty Smith business."

"Why? What's happening?" I felt an interested premonitory flutter; the Betty Smith problem, and that of the General, offered more interest than did Agatha's affair with Royce, I thought.

"Well, she just goes on pushing it, and the lawyer sounds scared and mad at the same time. I'd rather just give her the money, but he won't let me. Actually I can't help feeling sorry for her. The General *did* promise things and then wouldn't come through, all the time. One of his tricks."

Agatha seemed on the verge of saying more, and then did not. She might have been going to recount what I myself had often witnessed: all the times he said he would come to see her and then did not, at St. Margaret's, and a couple of birthdays that he forgot entirely. Legitimate sources of pain, I thought, and hard to forget—I knew this although my own mother had been very kind and reliable in those ways. But I had had lovers who forgot about birthdays, were mean at Christmas. Agatha would not have allowed herself that sort of self-pity, though; instead she felt sorry for Betty Smith. And in a way I did too. He was such a total bastard, the General was. I wondered if maybe Betty Smith was a little like me; that is to say, addicted to even the most miserable forms of love. But probably she was not—not like me; I would never have instigated a lawsuit. Or perhaps someone had told her to?

Suddenly switching topics, in a resolute, pulled-together way, Agatha said, "Royce is terribly worried about Ruth."

"Oh, really?" I regretted the change of direction.

"Well, it's dangerous where she lives. You know, out on Pine. He thinks she's asking for trouble. A kind of suicide."

I did not say, What a vain man, to think that his wife would want to kill herself without him; but that is what I thought. And I also thought it was very self-indulgent of Royce to confide in Agatha his worries over Ruth.

And—how censorious I was becoming! It was as though, having recovered from my own propensity for troubled love affairs, even cruel lovers, I didn't want anyone else to have them either; I was a reformed drunk, an ex-junkie.

As for dangerous places: what neither of us could have known, Agatha nor I, was that the very garish restaurant in which we then sat, enjoying our Mongolian lamb, some months hence would be the scene of a ghastly shoot-out, a Chinese gang war, five dead and seven wounded.

What I mean is, anywhere is dangerous.

Maybe out of a mutual, unspoken realization that talking about Royce, or Ruth, was almost impossible, Agatha and I spent the rest of the evening on Betty Smith. And the General.

"What in God's name do you think they were doing in Chile?" I asked.

Agatha took the question seriously, and slowly. "It *could* have been innocent tourism," she said. "He was great on keeping up with old army buddies. I guess that's one thing the army's good for, making permanent buddies. Maybe some other old Point person lived down there."

"Maybe some old buddy died and left him a lot of money." I was trying to be helpful, to aid her in making the whole thing sound innocent. Much as I disliked the General, dead or alive, everything about him, the idea of a full-scale investigation was a little scary, especially the ways in which Agatha would be involved in it.

However, despite all the cheery whitewashing things I was saying, I couldn't help thinking: Suppose, on the other hand, the General was guilty as hell? Suppose he was sent down there by the C.I.A., I.T.T., Rockefellers—to see about killing Allende? It could even have been his own idea, hatched out in his Pentagon office. Maybe he went down there to pay off the people who finally did it.

I wondered just how that would work. What exactly

would be said in the preliminary conversations—what words used? And how would they ever, actually, get down to the brass of it: here is so much money, he must be dead by such and such a date. Does all this happen in a bar, a coffee shop— a phone booth? Is the money in an expensive briefcase, or shabby envelopes?

And then how would the General be paid? With laundered money, naturally, but *how?*

Flickering scenes of all those activities ran through my mind like old newsreels.

I imagined the General, white suit and Panama hat, at a sidewalk café with "Betty," who would have to be a bouffant blonde.

Agatha interrupted these Graham Greene fantasies to say, in a sad thin voice, "I really wish I weren't in love with Royce."

"Oh?" All in all, I was a little startled, and I thought, What an odd thing for Agatha to say. She was never so direct, nor so self-revealing.

"It can't work out," she said. "There's no way for it to end well. Whatever 'ending well' means, I don't see that in our future." Her voice cracked with the effort at irony; I've never known anyone who had so much trouble talking about herself.

"It could work out," I told her. "When things settle down. You could even get married or something."

Agatha turned dark red, so that I saw for the first time how much she would have liked to marry, to have the calm and settled life that marriage, a Christian marriage, is supposed to promise.

But, "It would never work," she said.

18

"This is Stacy," said a soft voice over the phone, early one morning. For several minutes no face came to my mind to accompany the voice, and then I saw the whole tall blond vacuous person, Stacy, at Ruth and Royce Houston's lunch party. Stacy Page, presumably the former lover of Royce.

It was a strange conversation that we had, almost as strange as the fact of hearing from Stacy at all.

She knew I was terribly busy with Agatha's house, she said, but she was just terribly unhappy with her place in Belvedere, and would I possibly—could I maybe just come over and look at it?

My first instinct was to ask, Why me? Why not Michael or John or Bob? But then I knew why: someone, probably Agatha, or maybe even Royce, if they still communicated, had said that I was not available for local work, and that was enough for Stacy: it had to be me. I knew this because almost exactly the same thing had happened a couple of times before; in New York too I had had a reputation for being in a general way not available, preferring to choose clients for my own eccentric reasons, among which large sums of money were, perhaps foolishly, absent. For a certain kind of woman this sets off a sense of violent urgency: you become the person who is essential to her happiness—this is true especially of very rich women, with their restless wandering greed. And so I was beyond being flattered by Stacy's whim. It had nothing to do with me, certainly nothing to do with any skill of mine.

But in Stacy's case, what I had to recognize as a lingering attraction to Royce Houston on my part, and thus a curiosity about him, made me also a little curious about Stacy: could she possibly be as one-dimensional as she appeared? And so, from this quite questionable motive, I agreed that I would come over to Belvedere some morning to look at Stacy's house.

Settling on the right morning became more difficult than one would have thought, however. Stacy seemed to have a great many "appointments," and although she insisted that none of them was at all important, still they took up her time. And I had a few appointments of my own: with a highly recommended—by Tony—cabinetmaker, and with Agatha, for a tour of Jackson Square—she would hate everything she saw, I knew that. And I was going to Caroline's to see about the sculpture.

We finally agreed on a rather early morning hour, because Stacy's maid was off that day, and she was having friends for lunch. I was glad about the lunch, being quite sure that I did not want to spend a lot of time with Stacy, and that would let me out.

I had a very hard time with directions, going to Stacy's, up at the top of Belvedere Island. Streets were suddenly one-way, or they changed their names mid-block. Occasionally my anxiety over the time would be interrupted by a brilliant view down to the Bay: small boats and bright water, the gentle green shape of Angel Island. Or I would notice a wonderful house, some quasi-Maybeck, old and dark-shingled, surrounded with ancient shrubbery. But mostly I worried about being late, as though it mattered. And how I wished that I were not such a total slave to time; maybe punctuality is my substitute for tidiness.

At last I did find Stacy's house, and at the sight of it I almost turned around again; I wanted to leave and make a phone call from somewhere saying that I had got hopelessly lost, that by now it was too late for me to come, which was almost true—I was so daunted by the size and splendor of that house. Windows, balconies, decks, expanses of wood and steel and glass, and on such a scale! It was the sort of house that makes my imagination go dead, and in another way my heart dies too: I don't really believe that anyone should live in such a house. I am sure that it deforms the spirit.

Certain that I was making a mistake, I rang the bell anyway, and I heard, far within, a long discreet echo of chimes.

The tall blonde young woman who came to the door confused me: I had got the address wrong, after all?

She smiled, really a grin, and she said, "You don't know me without my eyes on, do you? I'm Stacy. Hi, Daphne."

We shook hands, and I saw that what she said was quite true; without all that eye makeup she was another person. She looked younger, and somewhat timid, and wearier, tired of it all.

She said how nice of me to come, and then I followed her into one of the largest and least attractive houses I had ever seen. The basic problem was simply that everything was much too big: huge windows, massive beams across the ceiling, a giant sofa, large chairs around a baronial oak coffee table. And everything there had been made to order: that was instantly clear to me; you don't just find stuff like that at Sloane's, I knew, and I knew too that it must have cost the earth.

Unutterably depressed by the house, I turned to Stacy, who was asking me if I would like some coffee. I said that indeed I would, and, not wanting to be alone in that awful awesome room, I followed her into the kitchen.

But there again, everything was oversized, more stainless steel than I had ever seen before. More formidable machines.

Rather plaintively Stacy said, "It's just never felt right to me."

God knows I saw what she meant. I was curious, too, about who had "done" the house—done this to Stacy—but I managed not to ask. Certainly it was partly an act of pure hostility; no human woman could have functioned happily in that kitchen—nor, really, in that house. It was all Stacy could do to pull together two cups of instant coffee, which we took into the living room.

We sat down, and then immediately, simultaneously, we both glanced down at our watches, which made us look at each other and smile: two time slaves who had recognized each other. I said again how sorry I was to be late, and Stacy, lying exactly as I would have done, said that it didn't really matter at all, "except for lunch," she murmured.

I had begun to like her a little, which was a surprise. For one thing, the Stacy I was seeing now, and liking, was totally unlike the woman I had met at the Houstons' party. This un-madeup Stacy was direct and friendly, a little shy, whereas the "social" Stacy was in constant flirtatious motion, batting those vacuous blue eyes—that today, unadorned, looked considerably less vacuous. Two Stacys, then: one for men, another for women friends. One Stacy believing that men won't like her unless she goes into a sort of frenzied dance, and that being liked by men is the ultimate value; the other Stacy allowing herself to be warm, to seem slightly insecure. The pattern was depressingly familiar, and I thought how nice it would be if women did not have to do that any more. Maybe younger ones don't?

I thought, too, of the odd sexual tastes of Royce Houston; from Stacy to Agatha seemed a very broad jump indeed. And then there was Ruth, whom presumably he had at one time liked. The possibility occurred to me that Royce could be the kind of man who always needs to have two women balanced in opposition to each other—satisfying conflicting needs, I guess. Derek had been like that; probably he still was. All the other girls, his strayings from me, whose characteristics he so clearly sketched out for me, had all been as unlike me as possible, as though chosen at least partially for that reason—small blondes as a sort of rebuke to my darkness, my large size. But as well as being a rebuke, and certainly hurtful, this balance of women, this duality in love, of course serves to prevent a real intimacy with either woman. Looking at Stacy, and thinking of Agatha, I very much hoped this not to be the case with Royce.

Stacy interrupted all this speculation to articulate what was almost exactly my own impression of her house. "It's just so big," she said. "I'm absolutely dwarfed by everything. When I bought it, it looked like a bargain, I guess, and then I got absolutely carried away. I got Chuck to do it for me"—Chuck?—"and of course since he doesn't do much residential work I was flattered, but I tell you, by the time it was over I absolutely hated him. Hughie tried to help—I think you met him at the Houstons'—but by then it was really too late, it was too big for any of us."

Too big for me, I thought but did not say, not just yet. I just said that yes, it was awfully big.

"A lot of gay men I really like," said Stacy. "Some of my best friends," and she laughed. "But Chuck: every time we were together I thought he was trying to say that if he was a woman he sure would be better at it than me."

I had often had the same perception, and had been quite hurt by it; back in the distant Fifties, when "womanliness" was touted as being such a revered and crucial quality, none of us could stand to be accused of lacking in it. And "gay" men did sometimes seem to be saying just that, especially when we were in competition with each other, or felt ourselves to be. Some decorators can be really vicious in that way, and I often had thought that they went into the field for just that reason, to show women how superior they were at supposedly female preoccupations. In any case, I knew exactly what Stacy meant about "Chuck."

"Since my divorce it's been worse, of course," said Stacy. "It's all even bigger than it was."

Looking about the indeed unbearably large room again, I saw that the mammoth windows were surely its worst feature; those huge brilliant views of sky and water and trees, boats and islands, all that intruded into the room—it was overwhelming. I asked, "Have you thought about draperies? I think they'd help."

"Really? But Chuckie said we couldn't, possibly."

I explained in a general way about Austrian shades, which is what had come to my mind; they would be just possible for those giant apertures, and I mentioned the natural linen—Calvin—that I had also thought of.

Although I almost never give out this sort of offhand advice.

Stacy was delighted, and disproportionately grateful. When could I start?

I suggested that we both think it over for a couple of days, at least.

And then I had another idea—this too being quite out of character for me. "Maybe if you had a small room somewhere in the house of your own," I said. "Furnished your own way."

Well: Stacy was enchanted. Actually, she said, she did do some watercolors sometimes. When she and her husband had lived in San Francisco, in the flat on Jackson Street, she used to do needlepoint, mainly because that was a sort of fad among people she knew, but she had decided that needlepoint was ridiculous—I couldn't have agreed more—and now she did watercolors. The point being, all she needed was a small studio room, just for herself and her work. But she had never had a *clue* what to put in it. "Maybe," she said, "maybe we could have lunch sometime? And then go to Jackson Square and look around?"

I said yes, of course we could, and then realized that I had entirely lost track of the time. I stood up, meaning to take my leave. Stacy had realized the same thing at the same time; she was suddenly very flustered and began to walk quickly ahead of me, toward the front door.

Too late: the chimes sounded, her guests—or guest—had arrived, and there was nothing for Stacy to do but open the door and admit—Royce Houston.

Fortunately, I guess, he saw me at the same time he saw Stacy, so that whatever their greeting might have been otherwise was headed off. But still it was awkward. Very.

At least Royce did not pretend that he had just dropped by; I gave him a certain amount of credit for that. Nor did Stacy pretend not to have expected him. But we both knew that given his supposed commitment to Agatha, my friend, he should not have been there, even if the implications of his presence were misleading—and I do not for an instant believe that they were: I am sure that a romantic lunch, *à deux*, was their intention.

Royce that day looked particularly wonderful, so big and blond, so *Californian*, a mountain lion, down from the tawny hills.

I got out as soon as I could, but not before Stacy had

gone into her "feminine" act; even saying goodbye to me, she twitched and fluttered.

I think I have heard about women wondering whether or not to tell a friend about an unfaithful man—a question for Dear Abby, I would think; and once a woman "friend" did tell me about an affair of Derek's. Maybe irrationally, this made me hate her much more than I did Derek.

I didn't wonder for an instant about telling Agatha where I had seen Royce: of course not, absolutely not, never.

It depressed me quite a lot, though, as well as making me angry. I drove across those lovely hills, still green despite the drought, with terribly lowered spirits. And the view of the Bay was especially beautiful that day, in the unnatural midwinter heat: I wondered what on earth I was doing in California, with my sad and aging dark heart, in the gorgeous land of the young and blond. Agatha and I should both leave, I thought then; clear out, the two of us. Royce and Stacy could have their California.

Being low-spirited in California is hard on a basically Puritan conscience like my own; you are not only depressed but you feel guilty about it, as though you had been ungrateful to generous Nature, who had placed such a bounty of beauty there before you. I sped over the hills, down to the pretty town of Sausalito and through it, speedily. Crossing the bridge, I could have been racing toward a lover, instead of just away from the sight of a beautiful day.

Back home, back in Agatha's house, I was grateful for the shutters, the lack of views. For privacy.

Predictably, I guess, as I worked without much interest on a set of drawings for the upstairs room, I became prey to the most violent longings to be somewhere else. Visions of once-loved scenery paraded across my inner consciousness: I saw Portuguese beaches; a tropical rain forest in Mexico; Fifth Avenue, across from Central Park; bridges across the Arno, from a Florentine balcony, and at last I saw Paris, the last and loveliest city.

Once, when I was actually in Paris, I took one of those excursion boats that go down the Seine; they start not far from Concorde and go down along the Left Bank to the Ile de la Cité, past Notre Dame, around the Ile Saint-Louis and back again to the Right Bank, as far as the Trocadéro. As I now retook this trip, imaginatively, the view that most moved me was that of the far side of the Ile Saint-Louis: the thin bare poplars against the old stones of beautiful tall houses with leaded windows, entrancing walled gardens.

Twenty years ago I had walked there with Jean-Paul, and I had exclaimed, "Oh, this is where we should live together! This is the most beautiful—"

He laughed. "You also pick by far the most expensive. In that house"—he narrowed his blue eyes speculatively—"I believe is the home of the Prince of Paris."

The prospect of never living on the Ile Saint-Louis of course did not bother Jean-Paul at all, but I think that he minded for me; and at that time I had no way to tell him that I was not serious. I didn't care at all where I lived, I didn't really care about anything but him. That was the absolute truth of it, but had I made the statement, I think he would have found such total dedication to himself quite as alarming as my supposed desire to live in fancy places.

But maybe I should have said it anyway. He might as well have known.

And now, twenty years later, I still felt so strongly for Jean-Paul, and for all that I had missed by not spending my life with him, that I could hardly bear it.

19

If you happen, as I do, to be frequently depressed at Christmastime, you can even come to be bored by that depression, and recognition of that boredom can almost function as a cure: how tiresome to feel low just then, along with everyone else. It is not just the fact of Christmas, though, that I find so disheartening, not being especially plagued by bad memories of that holiday. It is rather a literal seasonal sense that makes me sad—if you take the winter solstice seriously, Christmas becomes the nadir of the year. I see the months and weeks before Christmas as a tumbling downward into darkness and cold. And once Christmas is over, I think it should be spring; January snow is always a surprise, and very unwelcome.

However, allowances for all my private superstitions notwithstanding, the Christmas I spent in California was particularly difficult; it was full of terrible, violent news, as well as the more ordinary forms of dreariness.

Crazily enough, in early December, I began to be unhappy about Tony, what was going on between us. Or, rather, not going on. I was still glad, on the whole, that we had never fallen into bed together, although I was afflicted with sexual fantasies, sometimes vivid dreams of sex with Tony. Rather like Lady Brett giving up her bullfighter—with the marked difference that I had not had Tony to give up—I had "felt good" about it. But now, near Christmas, it seemed to me that we were not only not making love, we were hardly speaking. He did his work in a new, glum way; he barely smiled. And of course I took this personally: he was tired of the job, or, much worse, he was aware of my sexual interest —he somehow knew about those dreams—and was definitively turning me down. It was not I who had said no, after all.

One problem, of course, was that I still saw him all the time; there he was in my house—in Agatha's house—at work, attractively lithe and brown, in his tight clean jeans. He had one of the prettiest asses I had ever seen, so high and round, smooth, hard—or so I imagined it would be.

I was not only depressed about Tony, I was depressed about being depressed about him, which was quite an emotional setback, as I saw it. And at Christmas, as we rushed toward the bottom of the year.

Once Jacob, who although a junkie was probably my wisest lover ever—I haven't yet been able to think of Jean-Paul in terms of wisdom—Jacob said, "You really put a double-whammy on yourself: you worry, and then you worry about worrying. Daphne, you are hopeless." Well, Jake was certainly in a position to know a lot about double-whammies.

In any event, I felt that Tony and I were at an impasse. And I don't think it would ever have been resolved if he had not been the one to tell me about Caroline.

I had been out shopping, one balmy dry December afternoon, looking for sheets and towels, all that bedroom-bathroom stuff which I normally don't concern myself with for clients—in the trade it is called "accessorizing." But Agatha had said so despairingly, "Please, Daph. It's just something I can't do, or think about." I think she had been having a lot of trouble with Royce, of one sort or another.

Actually the rooms involved were not quite that far along, but since we had settled on the carpeting and fabrics, I thought I might as well see what was around. Also, in those days I was staying out as much as I could. Thinking that Tony was avoiding me, I decided I could at least make it easier for him, as well as for myself.

I believe now that I had really forgotten what season it was, which is easy enough to do in California. But there it was: *Christmas*, Christmas shoppers, tinsel decorations across the streets—what a terrible surprise. And perhaps because my own spirits were somewhat low to begin with, everyone I saw looked harassed and anxious, tired. I watched two women, possibly mother and daughter, fingering and then holding up a flowered sports shirt, for a man. It was expensive-looking, and quite terrible, and I imagined the scene that would take place on Christmas morning: the husband-father opening his present, pretending to like it but not going so far as to put it on and wear it, ever; the mother and daughter opening their similarly expensive and disappointing presents. And the rest of the spring, all of them working to pay off their bills, and those ruinous interest charges, 18 percent.

I stood it as long as I could, that Christmas-shopping scene, among the unbecoming, unseasonal fur coats, the crazy-looking tinsel in the sun, and then, before noon, I bolted away as fast as I could. I raced back to the relative safety and sanity of Pacific Heights, Agatha's house.

There in the kitchen was Tony, standing up and drinking a cup of coffee, frowning nervously. He had been waiting for me to come home, that was clear, and with bad news: the gravity of it was written all over his face.

He walked toward me. I thought he meant to put his arms around me, some friendly gesture, and maybe that had been his intention, but then he stopped short and blurted out at me, "Caroline's been beat up."

Sometimes my reactions are nuttily slow. I asked him several questions before I really took in what had happened. I asked: When? Who did it? Where is she? *How* is she?

It happened sometime last night, Tony said. Thomas found her on the steps leading up to her apartment; whether she was going in or coming out was not clear. No one knew who had beat her up, nor where, she was just lying there. Now she was at Mount Zion Hospital.

In the midst of hearing all this, I suddenly felt a jolt of cold terror, horror, fear. Lovely Caroline. *Beat up.*

I sat down at the table where Tony had put his cup of coffee, and in a dumb automatic way I sipped at it.

He asked, "Do you want me to make you some?"

"What? Oh, no. Thanks, Tony."

Outside, the unnatural sun shone on the glossy green leaves of a giant rhododendron, and on the new wood of the deck that Tony was making. I could even smell the fresh-cut wood, I thought, and it seemed a summer smell—all wrong.

Caroline. Beat up.

I stood up, and started toward the door. "I'll go over there, to the hospital."

"You want me to come with you?"

"Oh, Tony—*yes.*"

I drove fast and silently the short distance to the hospital. Once or twice I glanced over in Tony's direction, and he took my hand and patted it.

He told me where there was a parking lot off Post Street, and how to get there.

Within minutes after leaving the car we were inside the hospital, then inside an elevator, pneumatically borne upward. We got out at the appointed floor and began to walk toward the number of Caroline's room. A pale woman in a fur coat was walking in our direction, a full-length mink. The woman's face was pasty, wild-eyed, crazy; she could have been about to scream. And as we passed each other I recognized her: Ruth Houston. She did not even see us, I am sure.

This scared me badly, though: I wasn't sure that we should go in to see Caroline if seeing her had so deranged Ruth, her mother. I stopped and asked Tony, "Do you really think we should go in? Did you see her mother?"

"Oh, sure. Whitey told me a couple of weeks ago that he thought his old lady was flipping out."

So we knocked lightly at a door, and a soft voice answered, "Come in?" A question; it meant, who were we?

We pushed open the door and went it.

There were two white beds, two women in them, both with long brown hair. For a minute I was uncertain which was Caroline, and then my mind cleared somewhat, and I saw that the hair in the first bed was dyed and the face that of a very old woman, painfully lined. I started toward the second bed, the one beside the window, where Caroline lay.

She said, "Oh, hi," in an unfamiliar voice—sluggish, faraway. And then she said, more familiarly, "*Fuck*, I was afraid you were my mother coming back. All I'd need."

She looked ghastly. Purple, and outlandishly swollen. Her eyes were terrible slits and her mouth puffy and red, cracked, distorted. Nearly most shocking of all was her hair; it looked dead, a single dull drab shade of brown. What before had been so vivid and lively, bright.

I could easily have cried, just then, and so I concentrated on not doing so, on keeping control, keeping cool.

It was Tony who, in a choked voice, asked her how she was feeling.

"Shitty, actually," she said. "And my mother, Jesus: she comes to the fucking hospital to tell me that I've got to tell my father to take her back."

Across the street, glaringly visible from Caroline's window, was a funeral parlor. A blatantly tasteless, eminently practical juxtaposition, I guess. But how horrifying for someone seriously, perhaps terminally ill.

"She's gone crazy, she really bugs me," Caroline said, of her mother. She spoke in a far-off voice, and must have been heavily drugged, God knows with what. I could not help thinking how good it would be, in the long run, for Agatha if Ruth and Royce did in fact get back together.

I managed to ask, "Caroline, can I bring you something, anything?"

"No, just get me out of here." She twisted her mouth; she could have been about to cry, but she did not.

Tony went over and patted her hair; gently he kissed her cheek. And that day, in one of his oldest, most bleached-out brown work shirts and faded khaki jeans, he was as beautiful as a deer.

The woman on the other bed groaned and stirred; she groped about for something, something to grasp and hold, and then I saw the light flash on over her bed.

Becoming aware of her, this miserably sick woman, I thought too of certain absent people who were connected to this room, to Caroline: where were Whitey, and Royce, and Thomas?

Caroline said, "You guys really better go. I have to deal with this myself."

Tony asked, "Thomas coming by?"

"Yes. Later. Daphne, thanks for coming over." She turned her face to the window, and we tiptoed out, almost bumping into the nurse who was just coming through the door.

*

Back at Agatha's house, Tony and I sat across from each other at the table, over mugs of tomato soup, canned, which I had heated up. Into which we were both nervously breaking soda crackers.

We hadn't talked at all while I was opening the can, lighting the stove. And at last I asked the question that hung so heavily between us. "Well, who do *you* think did it? Someone she knew?" For myself, I already thought I knew who had so violently hurt her.

Tony looked miserably uncomfortable, but he faced me fully, heavy dark brown eyes raised to mine. "I don't know. I couldn't say," he said.

"I wonder where the rest of her family was today. Royce —and Whitey?"

"Oh, Whitey's gone up to Alaska," Tony said quickly. Too quickly? Had he read my mind? "He was going to go last week," he said.

Well, so much for my intuitive flash. I had of course been sure that it was Whitey, dead sure. I had almost been able to see and hear their quarrel, violent shouts about nothing, mounting rage—sexual in its intensity—until Whitey exploded, slapped her, hit her. Beat her up.

But if Whitey was in Alaska I was wrong, and probably I had just thought of him because I didn't like him.

With a small bleak laugh, Tony said, "Thomas. Mr. Houston's sure it's him that beat her up."

"Thomas? But he'd never—" Fucking racist is what I was thinking, meaning Royce. But I didn't talk like that to Tony; it might have scared him, I thought. "Stupid bastard" was all I said.

"I never saw a person look so sad as Caroline did," mused Tony. "She is brought down."

"She is. She really is."

It was true; Caroline's sadness went far beyond physical

pain. She must have known the person who beat her up, and if it wasn't Whitey, who? I absolutely ruled out Thomas; he would no more have beat her up than Tony would. I asked him again, "Do you think it was someone she knew?"

He frowned. "It sure looks that way. But you know, it could be some guy was a friend of hers three years ago."

Of course that was perfectly plausible, but I felt that Tony was holding back, not saying what he really thought, or not all of it. And as I looked at him, his smooth lovely brown face, I strongly felt that he too had immediately thought of Whitey, that he still did. Whitey *said* he was leaving for Alaska, that was all.

But I couldn't ask Tony anything further about Whitey; I'm not sure why—maybe because I was so sure that he shared my suspicion, and the idea was so terrible. Also, conversation with Tony had never been easy; words made him nervous, I thought.

However, I couldn't help saying, just then, "Tony, you are such a nice man."

I shouldn't have; he looked terribly sad, and he turned half away from me as he said, "No, I'm not so nice."

20

The Christmas season, having begun badly, got worse, and worse.

On Christmas morning, Agatha telephoned to tell me that "Betty Smith" had been killed in the underpass of a freeway, her car forced into an abutment by another car on Christmas Eve, the night before. This happened near Fredericksburg, Virginia, which was where she was then living. An accident: it was being investigated, an attempt made to round up and question other motorists who were on the road that night, who might have noticed something—but how to investigate something that happened between two large blind machines, on a dark cold night of alternating rain and sleet?

In any case Betty Smith was dead. She was no longer contesting the General's will, nor would her heirs, some distant cousins in Ohio; the lawyer had already made certain of that. The cousins, reached by phone, had said they "certainly didn't want to get involved in anything like that."

And so the sources of the General's money could not be investigated.

It was a crazily warm day, that California Christmas. It was as hard to imagine dark and cold, rain, sleet as it was to believe that Betty Smith's death was accidental. As Agatha and I talked about it, I was strongly reminded of the week before, when I had talked to Tony after we went to see Caroline in the hospital. Neither Tony nor I had really believed that Whitey was in Alaska; we both believed he was the one who had beat up Caroline, which was what I still believed. And so too both Agatha and I had strong and unexpressed fears about the fate of Betty Smith.

All this proliferation of violence was as frightening as cancer statistics were, and as out of control; it was as though the wars of the Sixties had continued into the Seventies, on another, hidden level.

How much better it would have been if the General had simply done what he seemed to have promised, and left all his bloody money to Betty Smith, maybe just a few thousand to Agatha—enough for a nice trip or, more likely, a sizable gift to some charity—instead of this cumbersome inheritance, her unwieldy house.

Even Royce seemed somehow, maybe illogically, a part of her legacy: an idle, rich and handsome man, who seemed to breed violence all around him.

"Well," I said to Agatha, over the phone, after we had discussed most of those things, "Merry Christmas."

"Yes." She made a small, despairing sound. "Uh—what are you doing today?"

I had been going over to Caroline's for lunch, but it was a loose invitation—"Oh, come anytime." She was out of the hospital, and she said that she felt great; she seemed almost to be pretending that nothing had happened, she had not been beat up, badly hurt.

Agatha's taut voice told me that she very much wanted to see me, and so I said, "Nothing, really. Why don't I come over?"

"Oh, I'd like that a lot. Actually, Royce was coming for lunch, but now he can't."

"Okay, swell, I'll be there in an hour or so."

I called Caroline, who said, almost exactly as I had imagined she would, "Okay, no sweat. Why don't you pretend it's dinner instead, and come by about six? Thomas and I are just sitting around."

"Good, terrific. I'll bring some wine."

The first thing I noticed about Agatha was that she had started smoking again. I was shocked: as young women we had both been heavy smokers, beginning with sneaked cigarettes in the basement of St. Margaret's. Then about ten years ago we had simultaneously given it up. At that time we used to exchange notes about how tough it was, what a hard time we were having without nicotine, and later we talked about how rewarding it was not to smoke, how strong-minded we both were. So it was a considerable shock to see Agatha walking around her small apartment smoking.

She said, "I know, I feel terrible about it. But things just got so difficult, complicated. And Royce smokes all the time."

"Still—"

"Daphne, please don't scold me. I'm going to give it up again next week."

That day I don't believe Agatha sat down, in anything resembling a state of repose, for the whole time I was there. She walked, she smoked, she fussed at preparing lunch, she spoke in fragments. I had never seen her so nervous—so unstrung, actually—and it was deeply upsetting.

We mainly talked about two people, about Betty Smith and then about Royce, but the sequence was always confused, and more confusing when Ruth came into it too.

"I just feel so sorry for her," Agatha said, and at first I did not get the identity of "her." "He said the newest wrinkle was some suggestion that she'd been drinking. Some office party, Christmas Eve." Then "her" meant Betty Smith, and "he" was the lawyer. Oh. "You know, even if she had been drinking, that doesn't mean that someone didn't shove her off the road."

"Of course not. But, Agatha, just because she was suing the estate doesn't mean that someone *did* shove her off the road." But actually I did not believe what I was saying for a minute: I was sure that the General, even dead, generated and perpetuated violence.

Agatha did not believe me either, but she was too distracted to argue. She said, "I'm so torn. In a way I really wanted there to be an investigation. If they'd really been able to find out where he got all his money, we'd know a lot, I think." And then, "Oh, Lord, I'm forgetting lunch." She rushed out of the room.

I too had very much wanted to find out how the General got so rich. I had even been afraid that it would turn out to be something relatively harmless, like clever investments. It would have been so deeply satisfying to have the General, though dead, publicly denounced as having been involved in the murder of Allende, in Chile, or involved in Korean bribery; having been an influence in the sale of arms to some big oil country. I fully believed—I still do—that his money came from one or several of those or similar sources. And now there was the probably innocent victim Betty Smith as dead as the General was.

I tried—again—to imagine in what terms anyone would tell someone else to get rid of a person, to see that Betty Smith had an "accident." But I could not imagine it, despite all my years of TV and movies and mysteries. I could not find the words for the actual conversation, which after all may not have really happened. But I am sure it did, and I wish I knew just what they said—not to mention who was saying it.

The lunch that Agatha had made convinced me, as nothing else could have, of the extent of her mania for Royce. She has always been a non-cook, not even trying very hard. But that day, that Christmas, she had made: oysters Rockefeller (on another day we might have laughed at the irony in that, the General having had at least two Rockefeller pals, about which he boasted), tournedos Rossini, artichoke hearts and endive salad. For dessert, some peaches with a raspberry sauce. "Royce really loves elaborate food," said Agatha unnecessarily.

Our conversation at lunch was mainly about food, not surprisingly: my compliments were interspersed with Agatha's running in and out of the kitchen.

She was in fact so nervous, so anxiety-fraught that she was virtually unreachable; my small attempted jokes fell flat, although they were in our usual language, our old private irony. I felt as though I were a new guest—or perhaps someone visiting a sick friend.

Over coffee we discussed Ruth's breakdown, its chief manifestation seeming to be her obdurate insistence that Royce come back, that they be married again. She often called him in the middle of the night, Royce told Agatha, and then she would carry on like a crazy person, screams and threats, long senseless monologues. "Royce says he thinks a lot of it is acting—she's trying to make him think she's crazy, so he'll have to do something about her," Agatha said. "But as I told him, beyond a certain point pretending to be crazy and being crazy are pretty much the same thing."

I agreed, but at that moment I was really thinking about Royce and Stacy; I was wondering how much he saw of her, if at all. For example, today: was Royce really taking care of Ruth, or could he be with Stacy?

With her coffee Agatha was smoking again, and I began to be aware of certain uncomfortable physical symptoms: a curious agitation in my chest, a flutter in my eyelids, a muscle in one arm that twitched. I wondered if I could be allergic to smoke, although that seemed unlikely; all Derek's heavy smoking had produced no such symptoms, and I had spent a lot of time, perforce, with other smokers.

Then, inadvertently, Agatha explained it: "I think she really is crazy," Agatha said, of Ruth. "I know because I can feel myself catching it, through Royce. I read a paper about that recently, in one of the journals, about people who transmit extreme anxiety states without necessarily feeling it themselves. I'm catching what Ruth is feeling."

As I was catching Agatha's anxiety, I then understood; my symptoms were those of an anxiety state, not an allergy.

Agatha indeed looked somewhat feverish, patches of red on each cheek, high up, her eyes too bright. I felt so badly about her, and for her, and I knew that there was absolutely nothing I could do. And I wanted to leave, very much.

Just then, mercifully for both of us, the phone rang; we both knew that it would be Royce.

After the briefest of conversations Agatha came back, radiant. "He's coming over."

Then I could laugh at her. "Well, you really won't mind if I leave?"

She laughed. "Well—"

We exchanged a quick kiss, and said Merry Christmas to each other, much in our old ironic way, and we parted on that note.

I had some time before going out to Caroline's. Once home, I left the car and started out for a walk, a tour of Pacific Heights, on Christmas afternoon. The city—that expensive, northwestern part of it—had never looked more brilliantly beautiful, more dazzling, more unreal. The huge houses were all so newly, cleanly painted, in bright pastels, each Victorian cornice shining and unshadowed. The lawns were a bright sharp green, unnatural and almost convincing. But it was Christmas, December 25th, the middle of the winter, the bottom of the year.

21

When I got to Caroline's, out on Clement Street, I rang the bell, and when at first no one answered, I had a strong impulse just to leave—an impulse that later on I very much wished I had followed.

But then I heard Caroline's voice. "Come on in, it's not locked."

I went in and there they were, Caroline and Thomas, both lolling across the mattress. Not getting up. I said hi, and went and sat down.

The room was a mess, the bed coverings disarrayed and dirty cups and glasses everywhere. From the west windows, some harsh final rays of the winter sunlight entered—no help at all.

Caroline and Thomas seemed to have been drinking for most of the afternoon, probably making love, falling asleep. They were not really drunk, but drink, along with their sexual exhaustion, put them at a certain remove from me. Conversationally they were very hard to reach, even had I been in a mood to make a stronger effort. As it was, everything I said sounded false and silly—"social," even when it wasn't. I asked Caroline how she was feeling, and I really wanted to know.

"Well, I've just never felt better in my life," she said, and in an unfriendly way she laughed. I understood that she wanted to pretend that no such thing as a beating had taken place, which was all right with me but a little difficult: there she sat, still badly bruised, although the bruises were lighter now and her hair was lively and clean and bright again. She was wearing the rough, many-shaded sweater which I had first seen her in, all those long weeks ago, at Stinson Beach.

Thomas looked very sleepy. His slant dark eyes were red, and he yawned a lot.

For every reason, then, I decided to make this visit as short as possible. God knows I wasn't hungry, after Agatha's mad repast.

In the meantime, by way of making conversation, which I seemed unable not to do, I asked Caroline if she had seen Tony over the holidays; he hadn't been around my house for several days. And this turned out to be my second ill-chosen question.

Looking mean, Caroline told me, "He's out hustling the Christmas tourists, I guess."

Panhandling, did she mean? I thought this was unlikely, and I guess I looked uncertain.

"Standing around the Hilton with his pretty ass stuck out," Caroline went on, more shockingly. But as soon as she said it, I knew; I felt entirely that what she said was true. And I thought, Ah, poor Tony, poor pretty Tony Brown.

Aching for him, I nevertheless asked, "He does that a lot?" I tried to sound much less concerned than I felt, but I doubt if I successfully hid much.

Seeming then to wake up, Thomas spoke thunderously: "*No*, not a lot. Jesus God, Caroline, you think it's any of your business? What a mouth you got." And then, as though he owed me an explanation, he said, "It's just something that Tony got into, kind of a habit, like, overseas. There was always some old guys, some rich old officers in Tokyo, Hanoi, fellows who really dug him. And Tony, he can't say no to no one. It was more than wanting the loot, or the coke, whatever they gave him. But you know, he's a really nice boy, Tony is. Just fucked up. Like who ain't."

"Oh, you poor fucked-over vets," said Caroline.

"Shut up, cunt."

Why is it impossible to leave two people who are having a fight? I don't know, but it is. I was dying to get out of there, and I was immobilized. I was thinking, Do they fight like this a lot? *Was* it Thomas who beat up Caroline?

Maybe to ease the moment—or possibly to explain why she was being so mean—Caroline said, "My mother was just here for an hour or so. Lord, you should have seen her. In her fucking *mink*, in this *heat*."

"She wears that *mink* to get your Dad's *goat*," Thomas said, with marvelous comic emphasis. "She acts like you sometimes do. Jesus God, one crazy family. You all could be a series on TV."

"You're right there," Caroline agreed.

By now the half an hour or so that I'd been there seemed very long indeed, and I thought it would be all right to leave. Which I did, as unceremoniously as I had come in.

None of us said anything about Christmas.

I walked home in the just-chilling early evening. It was almost dark, and fog had begun to creep through the streets, coming in from the sea. I suppose that walk was dangerous, at such a violent, suicidal time of the year, but I was too sad to be frightened. I was thinking about Tony, how appalling that he could put so low a value on himself.

My heart and my mind revolted from this new information about him. I would have given anything for it not to be true, but it surely was; it made perfect sense.

I reached Pacific Heights, those cold blank huge houses, these days with grilled gates, long windows heavily draped and barred. A big dog snarled as I approached his house and then, in the nuttily friendly way of some large dogs, who can't take their roles as watchdogs quite seriously, he pranced over to be patted on the head. A golden retriever, very handsome, with his noble head and long plume-feathered tail. I stood there with him for several minutes, making friends.

Once, years ago, with Jacob, at one of our winter beach retreats, we stopped to watch a big black dog who kept tearing into the ocean after sticks that his master, a young boy, threw out for him. The waves were high, slate-gray, and the water must have been freezing, with a stinging cold salt spray. I hated seeing the dog go through all that for a stick and a pat on the head, for that careless boy's just saying, "Good dog, good old Max." Jacob saw how I hated it—he saw everything—and he said, "Of course you hate it. It reminds you of yourself."

I realized that of course he was perfectly right, especially since we had just been talking about a recent suicidally stupid love affair of mine. It would have been just like me to rush out into cold water for a stick and a pat on the head.

And I now understood the ways in which Tony and I were alike, after all. Obvious dissimilarities aside, we shared an addiction to even the meanest forms of love. Which could explain the strength of the affinity I felt for him.

I got home unscathed, except by what was going on in my own mind. But I knew that Christmas was a dangerous time, a prime time for self-pity, self-laceration, corrosive memories.

As a guard against all that, I poured myself a glass of

wine in the kitchen, and I took the wine and a volume of Trollope that I was rereading up to bed.

But outside a mean wind pushed against the house, rattling windows, creaking boards and reminding me of everything I did not want to think about: Betty Smith and the General, Agatha and Royce, Whitey, Caroline, Thomas. Crazy Ruth, and Tony. They were not exactly a cheering group.

Going further back was not much help either: Jacob, dead; and Jean-Paul, lost to me, in Paris.

As I thought about those people, however, I felt curiously linked to them all, the living and the dead. We were in it together, somehow, together in this downward race to darkness.

At last, with a terrific effort, I was able to concentrate on Trollope, and I managed to stop thinking about anyone I knew, or had ever known.

So much for Christmas.

22

Once Christmas is over, I always imagine that everything will improve; there will be an end to that downward descent, and there will be spring, balmy weather, feathery new leaves and flowers. Of course I am often wrong, but never so wrong as I was that year in San Francisco.

Meteorologically, what happened was: the drought ended with a burst of cold dark rain, days of wind and wet which for a while, though uncomfortable, were welcome. But those dark watery days became weeks, an endless cold gloom in which the difference between night and day was indistinct. In an irresponsible way I began to long for a return of the drought, those lovely warm bright dry days, like a sharp longing for something illicit. I would guess that other people must have felt that too.

In the meantime, events in the lives of the people I knew in that city all seemed to get much worse, with a sort of terrible synchronism.

I had begun, at last, to do some work on Stacy's house. Together we had gone to Henry Calvin and chosen some linen for the living-room draperies, those impossibly high huge windows. And I had found a seamstress who said that she could do the job, and a drapery-hanger to install them. All that remained to put the work in motion was the most crucial step of all, the measurement of those monster windows, which Tony had said that he could do.

The appointment was made. As usual, with Stacy, there was trouble about hitting on a convenient time, but at last we found a couple of hours on a Thursday morning. It turned out to be the darkest wettest day of all, a day of angry black lashing rains and wind. As Tony and I drove up into the hills of Belvedere, leaves flattened themselves against the windshield, clogging the wiper; we couldn't make out street signs, and a trip that should have taken twenty minutes took over an hour.

At least, however, the difficulties of the drive and the state of emergency in which we found ourselves had provided Tony and me with a subject matter. We concentrated on the raging elements, we talked about the rain. I had been uneasy with him, or more uneasy, since hearing from Caroline and Thomas about his hustling, and even in my lively dream fantasies about Tony, sex had always been the only language between us. Thus the raging weather helped.

Stacy greeted us at the door. "Well, I honestly didn't think you'd be able to make it—what a day!" And she took a long look at Tony, and then went into her act: widening her eyes, dazzlingly; and, as I introduced them, she whispered his name. Preceding us down the hall, she twitched her narrow ass, that day in polished cotton.

I had wondered a little about just how Stacy would be with Tony—if the fact of his somewhat menial capacity and his curious color would put him out of her range, so to speak. Had that been the case, I would surely have liked her much less.

But batting her eyes, Stacy offered coffee—toast? Cookies, brandy, *anything?*

Tony had already got a look at those windows, however, and had seen the shape of his work, and he said no, he couldn't have anything; he'd better get started. Stacy and I sat together on the mammoth sofa, and together we watched as he clambered up to the narrow windowsills and perched there, with his tape measure and his tiny notebook. And we made conversation.

It was a funny scene, really, two big grown women, tall blonde Stacy and I, bigger and taller and dark, watching with our lustful-protective female eyes as Tony, diminished in scale by the size of those windows, climbed and clung like an especially beautiful, freakish monkey, a changeling. Probably Stacy would have liked to ask if I had ever been to bed with Tony, and if so how was he. And I could have said, Well, no, but I sure had thought about it. But neither of us said those things, and at that time I did not really see the humor of our situation, I was so tired of rain and trouble, and assuredly not ready for any more.

When the doorbell rang, it startled Tony, up on the window ledge; having almost gasped with relief, we both watched him recover. And as Stacy got up and went toward the door, I thought, Oh, Christ, it must be Royce again; why can't Stacy get her life sorted out?

It wasn't Royce. From the hall I heard another woman's voice, and from Stacy sounds that were falsely enthusiastic, falsely warm.

It was not Royce Houston; it was Ruth. Ruth Houston, soaking wet, in what looked like summer clothes, cotton, and with a bland smile that bore no relation to her condition.

She said how wonderful to see me, how wonderful I looked. I surely did not look wonderful at all, that day—and she said that she had just been driving by and it started to rain and she thought she would just come in for a minute.

All this in a voice as bland, as expressionless as her face, her narrow dark face that was so much like Caroline's.

But this was crazy: the rain had been going on for several weeks, and for weeks it had been too cold for summer clothes. And no one would be just "driving by" on Stacy's isolated and impossible street.

What Agatha and Royce had been saying was true: Ruth was mad.

Tony had stopped work and was staring down at Ruth, who had not noticed him, although they may have met sometime: Whitey's mom.

Ruth sat down gingerly on the room's least comfortable chair, tubular steel, which was probably a good choice, she was so wet. She spoke again, in a chatty, unnerving way, saying how nice it was to see us both, and then in just the same voice she said, "Actually I just had a rather curious experience. A person called me from somewhere, I think he said *Alaska,* and he said that a person up there named Royce Houston, sometimes called Whitey, was *dead.* Killed in a fight."

As she finished, Ruth looked up at us with the expression of a woman who has been gossiping with friends and who has just told them some news, nothing important, but a little hard to believe.

And then she closed her eyes, and in a slow, deliberate way she slid off her chair to the floor, in a faint—or I hoped it was a faint: she could have been dead of a stroke for all I knew.

More quickly than I would have believed possible—he must have flown—Tony was down there, squatting beside Ruth, his fingers on her pulse as he stared into her face. I was wondering how he knew about pulses, and breath, and then I remembered: of course, he had been over there.

"Just fainted," Tony said. "I think she'll be out for a while." And then, to me, "Jesus. Whitey." We looked at each other for a sad and helpless moment.

I was hopelessly confused, not taking things in nor knowing what to do.

Fortunately, Tony was clear on what to do, and he took charge. "Get a blanket, or a warm quilt," he told Stacy. "Just keep her warm and quiet for a while."

Stacy obediently went off, and Tony said to me, "I wonder if his old man knows. Royce Houston."

"Maybe she thought she'd find him here."

"Oh, that's right. Whitey told me he thought they had something going." Tony scowled with what could have been moral disapproval. "Jesus, what a family."

I wondered what his family was like, and I was pretty sure I would never know.

Stacy came back with a billowing, flowered comforter, presumably from her bedroom; gently she placed it around Ruth, and she said she thought she should call a doctor. "I actually know one who'll make a house call," she said. And then she said, "I wonder why she came here. Can she possibly have thought—?" And she blushed and went off toward the phone.

My own thoughts, or at least my feelings, were becoming a little clearer: Whitey was dead, and the next person for me to see was Agatha. Quite possibly I would have to be the one to tell her the news. I said this to Tony, and a few minutes later we left. Stacy had come back to say that the doctor would be there in half an hour.

Tony drove, and we talked very little on the trip down from Belvedere; we concentrated on getting through the rain and wind, the leaves, to Agatha's apartment—as though by just getting there we would save the world, or at least improve it.

Once I said, "It's almost predictable, isn't it. Whitey getting himself killed in a fight near a goddam oil pipeline, in Alaska."

And Tony said, "Yeah. It sure figures."

Only when we were crossing the bridge, on the way back into San Francisco, did it occur to me that Agatha well might not be there. However, a strong inner voice insisted that she would be, in her California Street place, and also that she would already know.

Tony asked if I wanted him to go back to the house; he could get some work done, he said. I said sure.

Agatha was indeed at home; she answered the buzzer as though she had been waiting for me. But when I knocked at the door and she opened it and saw me there, she looked surprised. "Oh. We thought you might be Ruth," she said.

We. Standing there, towering behind small Agatha, was Royce, who looked stricken, ravaged, almost destroyed.

No question, then, of telling them anything. They knew.

Stupidly I said that I was sorry. "I was at Stacy's doing some work," I said, not knowing how else to explain. "And Ruth—"

"Ruth called *Stacy?*" Royce was hoarse, as though he had been talking, or shouting, for hours. Screaming, maybe.

"No, she came by. Ruth came to Stacy's." As I said this, I knew that it sounded crazy, but just then I couldn't have invented another version.

"She's gone crazy," Royce said. "That's insane. She can't stand Stacy."

I said that I thought she'd be okay there, for the moment; that Stacy was getting a doctor to take care of her. No point in adding that Ruth was not only crazy but in a faint. Royce had already had much more than he could deal with, and maybe Agatha too.

He said, "Oh," and sat down heavily on the sofa.

Agatha and I sat down too. Whatever she was making of this, the Ruth-Royce-Stacy connection, I couldn't tell. All I could read on her face was the most intense tight-lipped grief for Royce. And love.

For myself, I thought Royce was exactly right: Ruth had gone crazy. And how pitiful, as well as mad, for her to go to Stacy with her grief. It was as though—dimly, crazily —she went there in order to *become* Stacy: a beautiful woman who was loved by Royce, a woman with no husband or children to plague her, alive or dead. She would not have come to Agatha, her old friend, a woman in many ways much closer to herself.

Looking at Royce, I could see, or feel, the most terrible guilt: all his fault, he would think, all of it—the torn-up family, Ruth's insanity, and Whitey's death—would lead back to him, to him and Stacy. If he had not "fallen in love" with Stacy, hadn't had that affair, not fucked her, none of these things would have happened to his people—so Royce would think; he would discount all the rest of the world.

I wondered if Agatha could possibly sort it all out for him, or even diminish the guilt a little, and for one instant I thought, Well, maybe she can.

A sound came from the kitchen, a sort of hissing splash, and Agatha said, "Oh, I forgot, I was making coffee."

Royce said, "Baby, do you think I could have a drink instead?"

"Sure."

Baby. I tried to digest that—but what an endearment for Agatha, who had been born grown-up, for whom no nickname was ever possible. However, I was in no mood to blame Royce for anything, least of all for questionable taste in affectionate words.

I went into the kitchen with Agatha, thinking that I

could be more useful in a domestic way than with larger issues. And that was precisely the case: she may have had a strong sense of Royce—how he was feeling, and how to give comfort—but the task of organizing a tray of coffee cups and making a drink was quite beyond her. I did those things, and it was good to have something to do; God knows we had little enough to say just then.

The drink seemed helpful to Royce. I could see a little color creep back into that big pale craggy face, and the slightest lessening of tension in his posture.

By then I had been in Agatha's apartment for about fifteen minutes, which had seemed a very long time. For one thing, there was the always odd situation of two women being with the lover of one of them, the man probably wondering how much has been told to the friend; and then there was the question of the feelings of the not-in-love couple, in this case Royce and I. I have to admit that I still found him terrifically attractive, even so nearly demolished, but I doubt if I impinged on his consciousness at all, especially not that day. Anyway, even in those extreme circumstances I felt that my being there was awkward; they should be alone.

God knows I was not being much help, and so I got up to go, having gulped down hot weak coffee. I said to call if there was anything I could do—of course.

Surprisingly, Royce looked up and said, "If you could go out and see Caroline? I'd really appreciate it." He added, "I just talked to her, she knows about—her brother."

And Agatha, "Yes, Daphne, do you think you could?"

I said of course, I'd go there right away.

It was on the way to Caroline's that the reality of what had happened began to get through to me, that Whitey was dead, killed in a fight, in Alaska. Up to then I had been so intensely involved with other people, thinking about Stacy and Tony, Ruth, and Agatha and Royce, so preoccupied with their reactions that I had not really thought about Whitey. Now, alone, driving the couple of miles through the rain to Caroline's, I did think about him, dead. But where there should have been an emotion I felt a dullness, a vacant space. This was my first experience of the death of someone I had known whom I had not liked, not at all. It was of course quite different from the death of a not-liked public figure: Senator X is dead—oh, good. In an abstract way I was even sorry that Whitey was dead.

I mainly felt sorry for Caroline, and, cowardly, I did not look forward to seeing her.

She answered the door almost immediately, and she greeted me with a small kiss on the cheek, an uncharacteristic and quite touching gesture.

Together we walked the length of the room, and we sat down on the hard wooden chairs beside her kitchen table, beneath the square window that was now a dark picture of rain, that leaked cold and wind. There was a strange new smell in the room, familiar but at first unplaceable, and then I recognized it: the strong clammy smell of wet wool, maybe of wet sheep. Moisture from outdoors had seeped in and permeated Caroline's wool; the hangings that lined the room now smelled.

Caroline looked pale and calm, powerfully controlled. For the first time I saw a look of Royce across her narrower, much darker features; I saw too how much stronger she was than her mother.

There were some dirty coffee cups on the table, and an ashtray full of butts. By way of explanation Caroline said that Thomas had just left, and then she said, "Jesus. Men. I'm about to give up on them all. Half the time they just don't know what to say. And even when they want to be nice they don't know how."

I made an assenting sound, but actually I didn't know what to say either, nor how to be nice to Caroline, any more than Thomas had.

"I just wish I didn't need them for sex," said Caroline.

Certainly I too had had that thought, usually at the end of some bad love affair; just after Derek, when I first came to San Francisco, I remembered thinking exactly that, and I said as much to Caroline.

"But I think I'm too old to start in as a dyke," she said, with a little laugh.

"Me too." But what a strangely timed conversation that was, all that anti-man talk, with Whitey just dead. Maybe Caroline thought so too, for then she asked, "Were you surprised about Whitey?"

I thought for a second. "No, not really," I admitted.

"Of course you weren't," she said, with a sort of triumph. "Anyone could see where he was headed. That's why he went to Alaska—to get himself killed. All that money talk he was giving out was just an excuse; he was just trying to sound like a normal person. Someone sane."

I murmured some sort of agreement, but I was impressed by her insight. So many otherwise smart people are so obtuse —myopic, actually—when it comes to their own families. And in this case such exceptionally strong feeling had been involved—I was remembering my first sight of Caroline and Whitey and Royce together, their intense rapport.

What was slightly alarming in Caroline now was her apparent absence of feeling, what shrinks call lack of affect. It was perhaps to elicit a more human response from Caroline that I added, "Still, it is terrible."

"*Fuck*. What's terrible was Whitey. And he was always the same. Only when he was a little kid it didn't look so bad.

But he was always too big and too good-looking and too rich, and a greedy bully besides. I mean, what kind of a person would enjoy Vietnam?"

"He did?"

"He had a ball, he loved it there. The high point of his whole fucking life." Caroline was clearly beginning a speech, I guess her final speech about her brother; she was gaining momentum and intensity ("affect") as she went along. "It's so easy to imagine what happened in that bar, in Anchorage, wherever," she said. "Whitey half drunk and thinking he could push some other guy around, only this time he picked the wrong one, a secret black belt, maybe, who broke his neck."

Then she said, "It's not like beating up your kid sister."

I heard that sentence clearly enough, and of course she was saying what I had always known, in a way. Still, it took a while to sink in. During that minute, I must have been staring at her, with God knows what written on my face.

In a soft voice she asked me, "You knew that, didn't you?"

"In a way. I *thought* so."

"Sure, of course you did." Her voice got very high and tight, wound up. "He came over, drunk, and wanted some more money for booze. And I thought, Shit, for once I won't give him any money. At first he was sort of kidding around about it, playing he was slapping me around. But then he really got into it, maybe because I said I didn't like it. It was like he'd always wanted to see how hard he could hit me."

"Jesus Christ." What I was feeling was certainly not surprise; I *had* known. Still, hearing about it and being able to easily visualize the whole scene was horrible.

Then Caroline said, "Daphne, you're a really nice woman. You were nice to come over." She sighed, and then she looked at me directly and said, very softly, "I think I'd better spend some time by myself right now. Okay?"

At the door we exchanged another friendly kiss, and I went back out into the rain.

Well, the truth was, I hadn't surely known that Whitey was the one who beat up Caroline. I had just darkly and strongly suspected that to have been the case.

But now, with my suspicion confirmed, I felt—maybe crazily, surely irrationally—that a couple of my other strongest and darkest ideas had been corroborated.

Whitey had beat up Caroline, and that to me meant, as I had also believed all along, that the General had got his money from murderous right-wing Chileans, or the I.T.T., or some combination thereof. And Betty Smith was murdered so that no one would ever find out.

And I am still convinced of both those facts, although by now it is truly impossible to find out for sure.

Part Two

23

The next few weeks at least were relatively calm. We all may have been in something of a state of shock—we oddly assorted people, my California nucleus. I know that I was. All that violence, which on the surface had nothing to do with me, had nevertheless been powerfully disturbing; I had been deeply upset by Caroline's being beaten, upset in another way by Whitey's ugly death. Even by Betty Smith's murder-accident. And the news about Tony had been in its way quite shocking too, his being in effect a male prostitute. Beautiful Tony!

And when Caroline finally told me that yes, it had been Whitey who beat her up, as I have said, all the other information fell into place, about the General's money and Betty Smith's death; it all fell into place and it stayed there.

From time to time Agatha and I talked on the phone, but we did not see each other often. She was much involved with Royce, and everything with him was very difficult, I gathered; I am sure that he still suffered strongly over Whitey.

No one had heard from Ruth, except for some curt business conversations that she had with Royce pertaining to the proposed property settlement, their divorce. Agatha reported that Royce had said it was really rough being up against a lawyer, which I found funny: I had had several women friends, married to lawyers, who had suffered from the same circumstance when they divorced.

Royce and Agatha seemed to feel that Ruth was all right now, functioning—not crazy at all. It was as though the impact of Whitey's death had jolted her back into reality, into sanity, as shock treatment is supposed to do. Royce thought she must be "seeing someone," a notion that both Agatha and I dismissed as old-fashioned, even sexist. But of course he knew Ruth much better than we did, and it turned out that he was right.

Caroline was okay, working quietly. I don't think she was seeing Thomas any more—as things turned out, she clearly was not.

Stacy, whom I continued in a mild way to like, was "into" various fashionable mid-Seventies activities: she ran, she meditated, she took tap-dancing lessons, and lessons in the cuisines of North China and Sicily. She bought a lot of expensive clothes. I don't think that she was "seeing" anyone either. In fact I saw her as a very Seventies figure, Stacy: if the Sixties were concerned with peace and freedom, free sexuality, the Seventies struck me as dedicated to consumership —although my so-called profession may have given me a somewhat biased view, representing as it did a sort of epitome of crazy spending.

Some sort of nonverbal friendship, or trust, seemed to have been at last established between Tony and me. We both worked hard, sometimes together, in Stacy's huge house, or in Agatha's, which now seemed home, since I lacked any other at the moment. Work, in fact, was all that interested me at that particular period; and maybe in my way I was a very

Seventies person too—temporarily asexual, earning too much money. Any other area seemed too difficult, and dangerous.

For a long time, it now appeared, I had been making a career out of personal relationships, and on the whole that had not worked out too well. It had led me, seemingly, to this network of violence and craziness in California. And since in a superstitious way I do not quite believe in accidents, I could not believe that my presence, there and then, among those particular people was entirely accidental. I was there for some purpose, which sometimes seemed to be a negative instruction: Do not go on as you are, it will lead to nothing good; you have to change.

The weather, too, had been conducive to little but work; the days were cold and bleak with rain, nights of wind, more rain. Everyone said what unusual weather we were having, but I was convinced that any weather in California would be unusual.

And then, as I had always believed that it should, the first day of spring turned everything around; it was, in fact, a great deal more disruptive than I could have bargained for.

March 21st. The sky showed signs of clearing; there was the lightest rain in weeks, or months, and the brightest air.

At breakfast I took note of the fact that I had now been in California for six months. Among other, more crucial issues, I had suffered six months of boredom-irritation with the local paper, which in an addicted way I continued to read, an awful paper being superior to none; once I met a woman who said she always read poetry with her breakfast, instead of news, but I have never managed to be so high-minded.

Was it Balzac who so frequently wrote about a "provincial capital"? I now saw what he meant. Local news always took up the first eight or ten pages of the paper: local politics, controversies over the preservation of "historic" buildings, local muggings and robberies. On page 11 or 12 you might read about the new independence of some African country, an election in Canada, a border skirmish in Israel or Libya, an atomic accident in northern Italy. And then there were the local columnists, with their unbelievable ruminations on the perfect razor blade, and on what San Francisco was *really* like thirty years ago.

Well, in the midst of all that, on the first day of spring, on page 17 I came across this item: ". . . the Regents of the University of California have announced the appointment of Jean-Paul ———, the distinguished French Socialist economist writer, for a special series of lectures at the Berkeley campus, beginning in June of this summer. . . ."

Christ!

My first reaction was one of the wildest joy: Jean-Paul in Berkeley! The most marvelous thing in the world, a gift, how fantastic! How wonderful the Regents all must be, to have chosen Jean-Paul, to have given him back to me, as it were. I wondered how many Regents there were. Could I send them all flowers? Letters of love? Jesus, how incredible! For an hour or so I could not stop smiling, idiotically.

But then, in a practical way, I began to think of other considerations. Just how would we see each other? I would call him and I would say—but what would I say? And suppose he should answer, Daphne *who?* And why did I assume that he would come to Berkeley alone, why not with a wife and children—or, worse, some glamorous friend. Why assume that he would remember me, if he did at all, in the way that I still so violently remembered him? He might only recall a big dumb sexy American girl, ordering a martini.

Or, even worse, he might only remember the scene that

I made the last time we saw each other, when he told me that he had to leave a day early, when I wept and carried on, when I said that I couldn't stand it—well, at the time I actually believed that I could not. But twenty years later, who would want a woman who behaved like that? For all he knew, I could have become a specialist in such scenes, which would certainly be less attractive at forty than it had been twenty years ago.

Managing for a little while to block that memory, that line of thought, I drifted back to the hours just before that announcement of Jean-Paul's, that he had to leave. I thought of our afternoon in the big lumpy bed, his attic room in the Place d'Italie, the louvered window open to a warm rainy sky, a gray view of tiled roofs, a church tower. And, in bed, Jean-Paul: his high white forehead, straight dark eyebrows and slant blue eyes. Straight nose, curved mouth and strong white teeth. Deeply indented chin. Strong smooth white young body, and that lovely cock.

I was stricken with a longing that was both violent and diffuse: I longed for Jean-Paul, and for Paris, and perhaps most of all I was longing for an irrecoverable period of time, for those moments of twenty years past. And as I sighed for all that, I decided it would be a serious mistake, our seeing each other again, Jean-Paul and I.

His being in Berkeley notwithstanding.

Twenty minutes away.

24

"Terminal decadence" was the phrase that Agatha used over the phone as she described the new restaurant we were going to try, and later, though I recognized the phrase, neither of us could remember its origin. It would have come from a writer we both admired, but that covered a lot of ground: Michael Harrington, Mr. Galbraith, Nora Ephron? In any case, it perfectly described the place to which we went—appropriately enough, owned by an Iranian who had left Iran, trailing his Shah, with his hundreds of millions.

The décor was dominated by huge stumps, real ones, from giant trees, and transported—at what must have been the most terrific expense: I know a lot about transportation costs, dealing with them as frequently as I do. And sandblasted—another mammoth expense—until the real wood, the real stumps, created an atmosphere of the most total unreality.

The high ceiling was made of wide wooden beams, also sandblasted to a shining, unreal pallor, and the floor was of broad, joined polished planks. Round wooden tables, wooden chairs. And in all the far recesses of the room there were giant frothy ferns in slatted redwood tubs. Agatha told me that she had read somewhere that the total cost of the place was over three million, which she could not believe, but I could believe it; I believed every terminal cent of it.

And in that palace of insanity, that tribute to rampant greed, self-aggrandizement, all those marvelous capitalist virtues, I was thinking of Jean-Paul—I had thought of nothing, no one else since reading that he was to come to Berkeley. I thought of him as Agatha and I talked, as we ordered and ate our expensive food.

What I was thinking, and trying to decide about, was should I tell Agatha that Jean-Paul was coming? I had not mentioned him, naturally not, since that night last fall after I had read about him in the column, when Agatha and I went out to dinner and I was so undone by those French songs. And so much had happened since; I would have to start at the beginning, to refresh her memory of how it all began.

I had thought a lot, in a general way, about the effects of "telling," and I had come to a few conclusions, the main one being that there *is* an effect; what is told about is altered, if only slightly, by the fact of the telling—of its exposure to air, so to speak. More precisely, its exposure to another person. A long time ago, when I was married to Marshall, I confided at last to a friend that in truth I could not stand Marshall; and after saying so I found that I could stand him even less. More recently, during my "relationship"—California word, a bad sign—with Derek, I used to make bright jokes about his terribleness, his cruelty, with various bright New York friends, and that helped; it did serve to diminish some of the hurt that I felt. I never talked to anyone about Jacob: how to explain the world's most brilliant, most talented and kindest junkie? Just after he died, I did call Agatha, who was already in San Francisco, and that modified the horror of his dying, just a little.

However, the actual, imminent approach of Jean-Paul made an odd situation. I absolutely did not know what to do, how to handle it. Very likely I needed some advice, I thought.

Most of the other people in that enormous room looked very young, but also nondescript, or perhaps that was an effect of the overwhelming décor. Their bright T-shirts and swinging flowered skirts and high stacked heels—that year's young-girl style—looked ineffectual and bland.

Agatha was talking about Royce, in the hesitant way that I had recently got used to with her. "I can certainly see why he'd want to drink so much," she said judiciously, as though he were someone she didn't know very well. And then, her voice tightening, she added, "But it's fairly awful to see. Like watching a person hit himself over the head with a brick, again and again."

Having had a couple of drunken lovers, and gone through at least one time of too much drink myself, I knew what she meant, all too well.

I murmured in a sympathetic way, I hoped, and then it occurred to me that maybe another good reason for telling her about Jean-Paul would be that of making a diversion. We were not getting anywhere with Royce, and my own feeling was that we never would. I thought he would get worse and worse, like the rest of the world, and all I could do was wait for Agatha to see it. And listen.

And so I said, "Something really strange has happened lately."

We had finished our salads. I ordered some fruit and cheese, and more white wine, and so, thus sustained, I began to tell Agatha about Jean-Paul. I reminded her of the beginning of the story—just as well, it all seemed new to her; well, God knows she had been distracted. I told her about the shameful time when I said that I had to have a martini, and she laughed at that, in a gentle, helpful way. I tried to say what I had felt about him—how, ridiculously, I still felt for him.

I did not say anything about his sex; contrary to a few

currently fashionable notions about supposed conversations between "liberated" women, we never talked in that way.

With the possible exception of Jacob, who had a wonderful way of hearing whatever I said, and often a great deal more, Agatha is the finest listener I have ever known. She takes it all in, saying almost nothing, but somehow giving what must be an emanation, an impression that she feels each slightest nuance of what is said to her, each shade of pain or shame—or even, in this case, although I did not quite say it, of sexual passion.

I went through it all sequentially, beginning in Paris, my London-Paris trips, and then the increasingly desperate, futile letters we wrote, up to and including my feeling of a final abandonment when he said—correctly, in answer to an unhappy letter of mine—that he was sure I needed a "presence." And I told her how I had felt, last September, reading his name in the newspaper column. And how I had felt two days ago, learning that he was to come to Berkeley.

I finished up, "So I just don't know what to do. About his being here. You know, it's not like deciding whether or not to go back to France and find him there, which is how I was more or less thinking last fall. But Berkeley, Christ! You can get there in twenty minutes."

"And phone for twenty cents." Agatha laughed, and then she frowned a little. "I do see what you mean. You can't just let him *be* there."

"Exactly. On the other hand, I could do just that. That would be the ultraromantic gesture. Like not ever revisiting an ideal place."

"There's that."

Thinking it out, as I always did when I talked to Agatha, I said, "I could even go over there, to Berkeley. Go to a lecture he was giving, or something. See him but not say anything, not let him see me."

"Actually you could do just that," Agatha said. "It could be a way to decide about seeing him. You'd look at him and then see how you felt."

"Agatha, that's perfect. You're wonderful, that's exactly what I will do."

She laughed at me. "Dope. It was your idea."

I believed then that was just what I would do; the plan seemed a perfect solution to my quandary, and we left it more or less on that note: my thanks, her depreciation of her own wisdom.

Coming out of the restaurant, emerging into the early spring night bustle of Union Street, seemed itself a minor liberation. I had not quite realized how oppressive all that expensiveness was, those blasted, imported real stumps. I said to Agatha, "I've suddenly got the most terrific idea for your living room."

She laughed. "I know, don't tell me. Stumps with real roots. Right?"

That night I lay awake in bed for a very long time, and in my mind I went on talking to Agatha.

Well, I will have to see him, that's clear, I said to her. Ridiculous not to, what a waste. If for no other reason, simple curiosity would force me to. Or complex curiosity.

But see in what way—as friends? Well, why not? I have thought sometimes that I am best as a friend. Never having been a mother, I don't know about that, but I suspect that I would have flubbed it, in one way or another. And my record with lovers is not commendable. But on the whole, with friends I am okay. Maybe we could, or should be friends, Jean-Paul and I.

Of course the real issue, which I saw that I was not too subtly skirting, was whether or not we should go to bed. And at one or two in the morning, whatever it was, that day, I saw almost everything against it. For one thing, I would be withheld by sheer vanity: he would remember the body of someone twenty, not that of a woman of forty, being in "good shape" notwithstanding.

Interesting: I did not consider possible changes in his body, and he was ten years older than I was. I think this is often true of women; we worry so much about our own aging that we forget that men age too, sometimes they get fat or scrawny, bald and wrinkled.

Much more important was the possibility that the act of love might not be equal to the feelings involved—my feelings, that is; suppose it should somehow not be superb, ecstatic—not marvelous? I thought then, and in my mind I reminded Agatha, of a passage in a favorite book of ours, Walker Percy's *The Moviegoer*, where two people who love each other in a most complicated way at last make love, I believe on a train, and the act itself is a failure. "Flesh, poor flesh"— something like that.

In a logical way, then, I had sorted it all out: there was everything to be said for seeing Jean-Paul, for our becoming friends.

And everything to be said against our making love. Again.

Except that I was sure that I would want to.

25

April, that year in San Francisco, was cold and wet. Sometimes I overheard the natives arguing about whether the moisture was rain or fog; the more patriotic view seemed to hold with fog, rain being an un-Californian phenomenon. Even Agatha, an adoptive Californian, would insist on fog.

I thought about Jean-Paul all the time, that spring; there was no moment when he did not occupy some part of my mind. And I came to a dozen conclusions, all conflicting and each to be abandoned, at one time or another, with the same enthusiasm which that very conclusion had originally engendered.

The least plausible idea, and the one which I furtively and hopelessly cherished, was that we would meet and fall in love again and live happily together ever after, preferably in Paris. Vividly I could see us there together, even as I accused myself of a total derangement, a failed sense of reality.

Curiously, and despite my overwhelming obsession, I was getting a lot of work done, on Agatha's house and on Stacy's. I spent days in Jackson Square or at the Ice House, or Henry Calvin's; I made decisions and wrote purchase orders and follow-up orders, and made phone calls, dozens of phone calls.

I had always thought that my work was more than a little crazy, those preposterous prices, and all that unreal, unrelated splendor; now it seemed to have got even crazier. For example, I called a furniture manufacturer in North Carolina to order some captain's chairs for one of Stacy's several decks; fine, yes, they could supply the chairs in the color I specified—in TWO YEARS AND TWO MONTHS. I could hardly believe it. The world could be over by then, I thought: nuclear "accidents," universal famines, cancer, earthquakes.

Or, at the very least, Stacy could have sold her house and gone to Paris.

In just that way, the thought of Jean-Paul pervaded all my other thoughts: of course it was I who wanted to move to Paris.

Then I ordered some carpeting for Agatha's wide front stairs; they were highly polished, slippery, dangerous—I may have been thinking of Royce in that house, falling drunkenly downstairs. My source in Los Angeles gave me a price, which sounded very high indeed. And, looking in my book, I saw that the price of that carpet, albeit a very nice one, in two years had more than tripled. My profession began to seem not only crazy but somehow evil, one more adjunct to a basically criminal system.

One afternoon early in May, Agatha called, and she sounded, for her, quite upset: Ruth Houston had disappeared, gone, no trace. If her office knew where she was, they were not giving it out.

Disloyally, I found myself quite unmoved by this latest crisis in a family with whom I felt myself so accidentally involved. I had seen Ruth only twice, after all—well, three times if you count that passing in the hospital corridor after Whitey beat up Caroline. In a human way I hoped no harm had come to her, but it was not as though Agatha had disappeared, for example, or even Stacy. And some instinct, from somewhere, told me that this too would pass; Ruth would be found, and she would be okay, and nothing much would change.

The real truth was, I guess, that I was getting tired of this obsessive love affair of Agatha's; to say that Royce was unworthy of her attention was to understate the case, as I saw it. Another truth is that the force of my own obsession, the force of Jean-Paul, had shortened my sympathetic attention span.

Agatha of course sensed all this, though I had tried to be polite, and she changed the subject, or almost changed it, to Caroline. "Do you know how Caroline is?" she asked. "Royce hasn't seen her for a while."

"No, me neither." Actually, I realized with a certain pang that in recent weeks I had hardly thought of Caroline. "But I'll call her, and maybe go out there to see her," I said. "Otherwise, how are you?"

"Okay, I guess. Working along as ineffectually as ever, hating most other doctors. Sometimes I think I'm in the wrong line of work."

"I know I am," I told her.

I did call Caroline, who surprised me by saying very warmly that she had been wanting to see me: could I come out for lunch the next day, Saturday?

I walked along Clement Street in the balmy blue May air, the first reasonable weather I had experienced in California, and I climbed the stairs to Caroline's apartment, where I had not been since the night she told me that it had been Whitey who beat her up, just after we got the news of his death.

Caroline greeted me in a friendly but very serious way; it was a greeting from a very busy person, someone with a high regard for the value of time. Together we walked down to the end of her long room, and we seated ourselves in those now familiar stiff wooden chairs. She asked if I'd like a glass of wine.

I said that I would, and she produced two glasses from the refrigerator, already filled with wine; no waste motion seemed to be the order of the day. And she looked almost too well-organized, her beautiful hair pulled severely back, her sweater a drab shade of green.

All that made me slightly nervous, so much efficiency. I felt as though I were being hurried along, and when I asked her, "Well, how've you been?" she almost interrupted in her eagerness to tell me, or maybe just to get the telling over with.

"I've been having this really rewarding new relationship," she rapidly told me.

"Oh, have you?"

"Yes, it's really interesting." She smiled, and I was struck with how happy she looked, more content than I had seen her for months. She opened her mouth to say something more, but at that moment the phone at the other end of the room shrilled out. Caroline said, "*Shit*," and went to answer it. "Oh, hi," she said, and she frowned.

It was not her lover, then, but someone she did not especially want to talk to; the tone of all her very short answers during that conversation expressed forbearance, no real affection or interest. "Oh, really?" she would say, from time to time, to what seemed a lengthy narrative. "Well, that's neat, I guess," she commented, at one point.

The length of her call did give me a little time for thought, and what I thought, for no identifiable reason, was: Caroline's new lover is a woman. For the moment she has given up on men. Or, less negatively, she has discovered women, in that way. And I found that I hoped two things for her: one, that she had chosen her lover out of love, not for reasons of theory or that year's bisexual fashion, although that last would have seemed out of character for Caroline; she was in no way a trendy person. The other hope of course was that the person was nice.

She finished her conversation and hung up. "That was my mother," she said.

"Really? She's back? Where was she?"

"In Puerto Rico, getting a divorce." The bitterness in Caroline's voice when she mentioned her mother was painful to hear, and she now looked somehow all disarranged, undone. The earlier look of contentment had vanished.

"I thought she still wanted to have Royce come back."

"She changed her mind very suddenly. It's a family trait." There was even more bitterness in Caroline's small laugh. "Now she's all divorced, and she's going to marry this really wonderful man. Of course he's a little younger than she is, about twenty years, but that doesn't make any difference, he's just terrific. He's a potter, in Mendocino, and she met him—are you ready for this?—because he came around looking for Whitey, he's an old army buddy of Whitey's. It gives them a lot in common, she says. Christ, what a thing to have in common. *Whitey*."

"How is Thomas?"

"I don't see him too much. He's trying to get into law school, and he's really into that. Wants to join the straight world."

She sighed, in a deep, hopeless way. The moment for whatever she had wanted to say about a new friend had clearly passed, and I let it go—it would have seemed wrong to ask her.

"Jesus," she said after a minute or two. "How did I ever get into this family?"

26

A week or so after my visit with Caroline, toward the end of May—*three weeks* before Jean-Paul was to arrive in Berkeley—I got two very disturbing phone calls on the same day.

The first was from a man who spoke poor English, and who muttered, but I managed to understand that he was a friend of Tony's and that Tony was in jail.

Tony was between jobs with me, so to speak; he had taken a few weeks off between one phase and the next. Actually, he had so nearly finished that this time off was simply a postponement of a few days' work.

Tony was so unhappy in jail, this person said; maybe I would write to him? I said of course I would. Tony was in the Hall of Justice, on Bryant Street.

I tried to find out more, but I had little luck. The friend did not know the name of Tony's lawyer, nor indeed if he had one; nor how long he was likely to be there. It did not occur to me to ask what he had been jailed for; I knew.

And the next day in the paper there was an article describing the arrest of several male prostitutes who frequented the Hilton area. Big news. A feminist "spokesperson" was described as saying what a great step this was, arresting men as well as women for prostitution. Personally I saw no reason to arrest either men or women for such a sad non-crime.

After talking to the friend I sat down immediately to write to Tony: how was he, what would he like or need that I could send? I must have sounded very maternal, but I couldn't avoid that sound, and in fact I did feel guilty and terrible in just the ways that a mother well might feel, I thought.

My second call was from Agatha, and it began in a by now familiar, non-startling way. We had talked a lot in the week since Ruth's call to Caroline, her announcement about herself and her marriage. Agatha had told me that Royce was more and more upset, was drinking more.

In any case Agatha had been having a lot of trouble—a lot *more* trouble—with Royce, and so when she began a sentence by saying "Royce and I have decided to—" I finished it quickly, in my mind, with *break up,* and I prepared myself to be kind and supportive. But that is not how her sentence ended; its last words were "get married."

Silenced—actually I was horrified—I struggled for something to say; finding nothing "appropriate," I began to babble, "Oh, really? Well, great, that's terrific, when?" I must have sounded as though Agatha were someone I hardly knew. And when I was able to think, I began to wonder if that is how it would be between us, a diminution, a diluting of friendship. It is one thing to discuss or even to complain about an ongoing love affair, but marriage is quite different, requiring more severe loyalty. And, once so committed, it seems undignified to complain. Or so I felt it, and I knew that Agatha would too.

She said, "Next week. It seems rushed, but why wait around? It will just be a small church wedding." Only Agatha could have injected irony into that sentence. "You'll come, of course?"

"Oh, yes, of course."

"In fact you'd better plan on being maid of honor—person of honor? Or maybe you'd rather give me away."

At that we could both laugh a little, and by the time we hung up I felt a little better, but not much.

Ironic coincidence: the next morning a brief note came from Derek saying that he—*too*—was going to be married. Amusingly, I thought, in view of his former habits of unwelcome disclosure, he said almost nothing by way of describing his intended, only telling me that her name was Monica Reddington, which I guess he supposed to have an impressive sound. Instead, to me it conjured up a strawberry blonde with slightly crossed eyes, very lanky, with a whinneying sort of speech. However, no doubt that was just a malicious wish; in any case, I was never to know what Monica actually looked like, nor to hear from Derek again.

On Agatha's wedding day she was truly, vividly beautiful, more so—at forty—than at any time during the years I had known her.

She was a wonderful exception, I thought that day, to the dubious rule that (along with other biological inequities, like menstrual periods and relatively more difficult orgasms) men, more often than women, get handsomer with age.

Her dress was a pale blue, almost silver, so that her blue eyes deepened and darkened. Her skin was pink and white, delicate. But mainly she just looked happy, an illuminated woman. Someone seeing her then, for the first time—and this must have been true for several of the wedding guests—such a person would not imagine for her a previously more than difficult life, early deprivations and loneliness—true disorder and early sorrow. A dead mother and a cruelly selfish, neglectful father, the late General. One would simply have seen an exceptionally attractive, intelligent woman—which of course was another accurate description.

Royce too looked wonderful: somehow larger, more shiningly blond than ever, and his face, like Agatha's, showed not the slightest trace of past grief or turbulence. He too looked purely happy.

They stood together in the sunny courtyard of the church, radiating love.

Caroline was there, of course, with a tall blonde woman whom at first I took to be Stacy; closer up, she was younger and much less fashionable that Stacy was. She was Caroline's lover, I guess.

Very curious, the relationship between Stacy and this family: at first, seeing her with Royce at the Stinson Beach party, I had imagined them to be married, and then, later, I had thought she looked enough like Whitey to be his sister. In any case, it seemed both odd and fated that Caroline should choose a tall blonde lover.

The other guests were either colleague-friends of Agatha's—doctors, doctors' husbands and wives—or Royce's friends. It was easy to tell them apart, the Royce-friends being so much more stylish.

After a while there came a sound of organ music, Bach, "Sheep may safely graze," and we all filed into the church. Without much ado, Agatha and Royce and the minister took their places in the transept, the music became softer and the minister began.

"Dearly Beloved, we are gathered . . ."

I began to cry.

27

A letter from almost anyone with whom one has not had a written relationship can be a real shock. Even after all the years that we have known each other, I have never got used to letters from Agatha; they are so trite and dry—so *boring* —so unlike her.

On the other hand, there are those rare people who sound like themselves. One extreme would be Ethel, whose letters were as stupid as her speech; like many semi-illiterates, she underlined a great deal, sometimes three or four times, for great emphasis—some editor must have had a terrific time with her prostitute novel. Ellie Osborne's letters were arrogant, with even a nasal sound. Jacob's letters were brilliant and funny and outrageous and kind. Letters from Jean-Paul were somehow heroic; his prose had a Miltonic grandeur.

No letters in my experience, however, would have prepared me for the one that came from Tony Brown, in South Lake Tahoe.

To begin with, it had exactly the look of a kindergarten exercise paper, and indeed the paper was lined, in that way. The very look of it made me sad, as though I had again learned something about Tony that I did not want to know. But probably this was just my own bias in favor of good clear prose. Tony very likely didn't care how his handwriting looked, nor that the only word he could spell correctly was the pronoun "I."

I did wonder, however, about California schools; or maybe all schools now are letting out people who can't write letters—which does seem a basic skill.

In any case, there he was at South Lake Tahoe, the gambling center, the best place ("bezt plaice") he had ever been. He was working for a lot of money on some condos ("condoz"); he was staying out of the casinos. He was fine. He would come back to San Francisco in August and finish up my work.

Well, some happiness came through with all that, and for that happiness I was truly glad.

28

In the weeks which soon narrowed down to days before the arrival of Jean-Paul in Berkeley, I did nothing whatsoever that was sensible. I did not call the Department of Economics to find out where he was staying, or if he was to come alone; and God knows I did not leave my name anywhere for him to call. I did not even inquire, as I might have done quite anonymously, about just where and when his public lectures were to be, although attending one of them was still my vaguely formed plan. I felt his advent to be so momentous that I did not dare breathe in its direction, not even over the phone.

But the scheduled day did at last arrive, and it was the most beautiful day I had ever seen in California, a pure blue and golden day. I knew that he must be safely here, on this edge of the continent with me; there was nothing in the paper or on TV news about plane crashes—no crashes anywhere, no accidents; there seemed to have been a suspension of calamities that day. And I was as giddily happy as if I were sure of seeing him again, of being with Jean-Paul.

I was so silly, so dizzy, in fact that I did not at all take in the significance of a letter that came that morning from my furniture person in Hoboken, Mr. Evring. I only saw it then as a very good omen, whereas actually it was considerably better than an omen.

What it came down to, the letter, was that someone from Bloomingdale's wanted a large order of an expensive chair that I had designed, and Mr. Evring had made for me, some time ago. Actually, a few months before this—when I must have been in the midst of some upset over Caroline, Whitey, Agatha or Royce, my California people—a former client-friend had written to ask about those chairs, of which she had one, and she had mentioned the Bloomingdale person. Mr. Evring now specified the size of the order, and he made his suggestion about my share—that most meticulously honest of men. Anyway, it came to somewhat more than a normal year's earnings for me; it was like getting a Guggenheim.

The only thing about the chair that made me a little uneasy was its very expensiveness: it would have to retail for a couple of thousand dollars, with all its carved walnut and glove leather and down; I had designed it almost as a joke, a parody of expensiveness. However, I had not counted on the mass production of my parodic intent; it made me wonder, again, about my own connection with inflation, and with an entire economic structure of which I disapproved.

But for the first time in my life I would have an income that I did not have to work for every day, an income that I had in fact earned some time ago. I did not in any immediate practical way connect this with the coming of Jean-Paul, which is to say that I did not make instant plans for trips to France. As I have said, it just seemed another most propitious sign, along with the lovely weather.

Everything in my mind, during those first strange days of knowing that Jean-Paul was half an hour away, was vague, and vaguely marvelous. I made no plans. I had stopped wondering about how or when—or even *if*—we would meet.

Whether he would know me, would remember anything of me. No more imagined conversations about whether we would or would not make love. I was simply and stupidly happy in my knowledge of his proximity. I was floating.

Agatha telephoned me on the day after the Arrival, and she even seemed to share my mood, although for somewhat different reasons. She too was foolish with happiness—though, being Agatha, she could not quite say so. She and Royce had been up at Tahoe, on what she deliberately did not refer to as their honeymoon; they had stayed in Royce's house on the lake. What Agatha said was "It was really pretty, all the time. The lake. Really pretty."

In Agatha's prim vocabulary "pretty" stands for terrific, marvelous, beautiful—in anyone else's overblown language. She would only use "gorgeous" as a joke. In fact we had once talked about "gorgeous," and we agreed that that word is to the Seventies as "beautiful" was to the Sixties, and we found great significance in the difference. Wouldn't any right-thinking person rather be beautiful? Anyway, Agatha sticks with "pretty."

She did not precisely mention Royce, not his name, that is; but she kept saying "we": we swam a lot, we hiked, we watched a storm. It was from Agatha an unfamiliar pronoun, making me feel strongly the presence of Royce. And I remembered the picture Royce had shown me of the small house on the blue lake, where I had never been, so far. At the time of course I did not know about my own week there, and so I thought about Agatha and Royce, married to each other. And I thought, Well, maybe they will work it out, and be at least reasonably happy with each other. Interesting how one's hopes for happiness, even for one's favorite friends, tend to diminish with increasing age and wisdom.

I thought too of all the blows that Royce had in the past few months sustained: his wife having left him—never mind how he felt about her, nor that he also had a girl friend; it would still be a blow. His son Whitey beating up his daughter, his adored Caroline, and then that same son being murdered in a barroom brawl, in Alaska. And then his former wife marrying a very young man. Was it possible for Agatha to counterbalance all that, as it were? After so much pain, to make him happy? For the moment, at least, it looked as though she could. As though she had.

"M. Jean-Paul ———— [misspelled, trust the local paper] the distinguished French economist, will present the first of a series of lectures on the general topic of Euro-Socialism, tomorrow night at 8 p.m. in Herz Hall, on the Berkeley campus. The lecture is open to the public."

This item sprang out at me from the paper, a couple of days after Jean-Paul's arrival, and one of the things that came to my mind was: Oh, poor thing, he just got here. They're really pushing him, getting their money's worth.

However, I was not surprised by the item; it was rather as though I had been given a signal, the one for which I had been waiting. And so, in a most disorderly way, I began to think about what to wear, and how to get to Berkeley. How to find Herz Hall, once there, and, almost incidentally, what I could conceivably say in the possible event of a confrontation with Jean-Paul.

Thus I had about thirty-six hours during which to consider possible ways of getting there, possible clothes. I thought of driving over by myself, but I might get lost. I could take the bus, or BART, but suppose I couldn't find a cab, once there? I could take a taxi all the way from San Francisco, which

would be expensive, but it might be the best way, after all—
but how would I then get home? And in the same way, dis-
carding one thing after another, I went through all my
clothes: new red blazer, old trench coat. My total illogic was
dizzying.

And I *could not wait*. During those thirty-six hours, I
learned the real meaning of that phrase. Had I known any
possible means of doing away with that time, the time before
seeing Jean-Paul, I would have seized upon it, but I did not.
I find Valium depressing, and I don't much like to drink during the day, except very festively, with other people.

I was stuck with consciousness. With waiting.

By the following night I was so deranged with anticipation, so weakened by vacillating fantasies and plans, that certain decisions came to me ready-made: just as I was unable to
eat any dinner other than a soft-boiled egg, so too I could not
have put on any but my most ordinary clothes, black turtleneck and jeans and boots, my old trench coat. And I could
not possibly have driven myself to Berkeley, or made it to
BART or a bus. I called a cab.

Only inside the taxi, as we crawled, it seemed to me,
across the nighttime city, approaching the Bay Bridge, its
murky yellow lights—only then did it cross my mind that I
was wearing almost exactly what had been my uniform in
Paris twenty years before. If I had meant to costume myself
as that Daphne of the past, I could not have done better.

At last we got there, got to somewhere in Berkeley, that
is; and the driver pointed to a building, through the fog, that
he said was Herz Hall. As I was paying him, I considered
telling him to come back for me at around ten-thirty, but
then I saw a lighted public telephone booth, and I thought I

could more easily call when I actually wanted a cab. Who knows? More than half an hour of seeing Jean-Paul might do me in, and I might have to bolt.

I was rather pleased, even, at the practical line my thoughts were taking, knowing myself to be in such a dangerously overwrought state. I could easily have left the house without my keys, or not enough money for cab fare, any of those innocent acts of self-destruction, but I had checked all those possibilities out, and so far I was relatively okay.

Another wise precaution had been to time my trip so that there would not be too long a time to wait; natural inclinations would have led me to arrive at least half an hour early, and quite possibly to die of anxiety in the interim.

Thus I walked into a large hall in which there was already a number of people, all waiting for Jean-Paul, the distinguished French Socialist economist, and the great love of my so-far foolish life. I sat about halfway down, on an aisle, both because aisle seats are generally better for excessively long legs like mine, and because I still had some idea that I might want or need to leave, in a sudden way.

The other people in the audience were mostly young, strange Seventies kids with trim hair and tidy clothes; even their beards were neat. Many of the girls had that frizzy-curled hair—a look that in the distant Fifties we would have done anything to avoid—and blood-black lipstick. I felt myself to be somehow invisible among them, a dim dark middle-aged ghost.

At last a tall, thin graying man came out on the stage— the professor chosen to introduce Jean-Paul, I imagined. He reached the lectern, and then he began to cough, and I thought, Oh, poor fellow. But then the coughing stopped and he smiled and said, "Please excuse," in familiarly accented English.

Jean-Paul. It was Jean-Paul.

I think that at the moment of hearing his voice I went into a mild form of shock, for literally, for the next hour or so, I heard almost nothing of what he said, just sometimes that worrying cough, which recurred, and a few scattered words and phrases. I have no idea where my mind was while he spoke, beyond being totally, dizzingly absorbed in his presence. But at least some part of my consciousness had gone back to those narrow, once intimately known streets of Paris, where with another, much younger Jean-Paul I had wandered, all those years ago.

". . . while, in actual fact, the only European unity, the only truly international movement is among the terrorists," Jean-Paul was saying—and then that cough.

It had to be jet-lag, or a cold, I prayed, thinking of course of lung cancer or, somewhat more romantically, TB.

During one of my few moments of coherence, in the course of that violently charged hour, I decided that what I was doing was quite right, after all; it was right for me to come and listen to Jean-Paul; and it would have been wrong for me to call or write and say that I was here, available, that for this season I was living nearby, in San Francisco. I would come to all his lectures, and between times I would study. Having always felt and sometimes said that I was a Socialist, meaning that I didn't think capitalism was working out very well, now in a serious way I would study Socialism. I would read Michael Harrington, David Dellinger, Gramsci, Hegel, C. Wright Mills, Galbraith. And, first off, anything by Jean-Paul that I could lay my hands on.

He coughed again, and with one raised hand he signaled that he had come to the lecture's end, all done. Wild applause began; he seemed to have struck off something even in those children of the Seventies, and in the other professors, wives, friends and visitors, like me. I watched as people surged forward to crowd around him.

Then I got up and left the hall, not looking back.

Outside, I realized that the one precaution I had not taken was to make sure of my bearings; now I was not exactly lost, but I was very confused. I wandered up a path, and realized that I had taken a wrong direction. But without too much trouble I made my way back to Herz Hall.

And there on the steps, was Jean-Paul. With a group of students. There was no way for me to walk past them without looking straight at Jean-Paul.

Who suddenly looked up—who called out, *"Daphne."*

As those kids stood around and stared, we hurried toward each other; not yet touching, we took in each other's faces, staring hard, and then our hands met, and held.

Jean-Paul, with more audience awareness than I possessed, turned briefly to the students. With a gesture of his head he dismissed them, saying pleasantly but finally, "Good night." That gesture, and those words, seemed also to dismiss the years between us.

29

We stood there kissing, like people famished for love—and for me certainly that was true. We stood blotted together; it is amazing that we didn't fall as we swayed, pressing closer to each other.

For a while all that we spoke were endearments, and words of incredulity. Jean-Paul especially could not believe it, my being there in California, waiting. And I could not believe that we were actually together, that he was real.

At last he said, "They have put me in a club. I have just this small room, but will you—?"

"I have a house. We'll get a taxi."

The luck of lovers: at that moment an empty cab cruised toward us; we hailed it and got in, and we began the journey back to San Francisco in the sparkling darkness.

On that trip, between our continuing, ravenous embraces, we did talk a little, about immediate things, not yet touching on the twenty years between and behind us. I explained how it was that I came to be in San Francisco: Agatha's house, my job.

Jean-Paul said that he would be in Berkeley for only two weeks, but that he had meant to spend the rest of the summer in this country, traveling about, a few professional engagements: more speeches, articles, meeting editors and activists. Well, for the moment the summer sounded like the rest of our lives.

He coughed, and he explained that he had "a little" emphysema. "But it is not serious," he said.

Sometimes, in the sudden light from a passing car, or streetlights, glaring bridge lights, in a flash I could see his face, and he had aged: there were deep lines and shadows, and his skin was drawn more tightly to his skull, but surely I would have known him anywhere. With my fingers I traced his forehead, eyebrows, the sockets of closed eyes. His smooth mouth, and sharply indented chin—as I had twenty years before. I could have wept, but happily did not.

Back at Agatha's, I led him into my—our—darkened house, into the kitchen, where we opened a bottle of wine, poured it into glasses and toasted each other, standing there.

In the strong kitchen light we looked at each other, really for the first time, and Jean-Paul said, "In my life I have never known a woman so beautiful as you." Well, I am sure that was not true; in the first place I am not a beautiful woman, nowhere near. Still, it was nice—if very French—of him to say that, and I took it to mean that he loved me. Still.

Of course soon after that we went to bed, and for the rest of the night our only talk was words of love.

One bit of conversation I do remember clearly, though.

"Making love is different after you pass forty or so, isn't it."

"Yes, it's much better."

The funny part is that I cannot remember which of us spoke which line.

30

After several days and nights of tearing back and forth to Berkeley, of trying sometimes to eat and sleep a little—of being almost always with Jean-Paul—I managed to catch enough of my breath for a phone call to Agatha; and I gave her a somewhat underplayed version of what was going on with me. How I was.

I can't have underplayed it quite enough, though, for at the end of my account she said, "Good Lord, that sounds totally exhausting. Look, why don't you go up to Tahoe for a week or so, after Jean-Paul is done lecturing? Royce has that house, and we're so understaffed at the hospital that I know I can't get away this month."

Well, Jean-Paul, after his lectures, had those other commitments, in other places—some, not all, of which he kept. When he did I traveled with him, to Chicago, to Portland, Oregon. We did not get up to Tahoe until August.

And that is how we came to spend our week in Royce's cabin on the lake, the happiest and most entirely beautiful week of my life—so far, but then I don't actually have the highest hopes for the rest.

A great advantage that comes with reaching a certain age is that when you're really happy you know you are, and you give thanks. As I said earlier, I had a lot of happy times when I was young, particularly during my sexy girlhood in Madison, but I was too young to appreciate how I felt, and too crazily in a hurry to get on with growing up.

It was a small house, set back and up from the lake, on a rocky knoll, among pines and poplars. The lake was clear and shallow at the shore, gently rippling over smooth brown rounded rocks—and cold: sometimes we waded out a little way; a few times we actually swam, but not for long.

There was a stand of aspens near the edge of the water, just above that level cleared space, where Royce had put a table, and that was where we ate our salads and wine and cheese for our lunches, all that week.

The house itself was of two stories, one room to a floor; the downstairs a combined living room and kitchen, upstairs the bath and the bedroom, our bed, from which every morning, when we first woke up, we could see the sun as it rose above the Nevada mountains, on the other side of the lake. And all day we would watch the changes of light and color, shifts from dark to light, blue to gold, on the mountains and on the water of the lake. We watched pale mauve-to-lavender sunsets, and small fleet sunstruck clouds. And that is what we talked about, for the most part. We observed and noted the changes in our immediate surroundings. We watched the small chipmunks and tiny birds that abounded in that place; we laughed at their scurryings and sudden stops to look around, and we put out bread crumbs.

We praised and blessed each other, for everything.

Otherwise, we talked rather remarkably little, and what I learned of Jean-Paul's life over the past twenty years came out largely by indirection; he tossed out pieces of his life like inconsequential objects, and I think that is more or less how he felt about it, being a vastly modest man. He told me that he had never married, partly out of conviction, but I gathered that there had usually been someone around, some woman.

In that regard he sounded a little like me. One woman he had lived with was an Italian movie star, who had died tragically, in a fire—I thought I remembered reading about that. He had spent a lot of time traveling, mainly to meetings, conferences. Vienna, Rome, Dubrovnik, a couple of times to Moscow, recently to Cuba. He had taught at various universities, and lived for some years in Bologna, in Montpellier—had edited magazines, published a lot of books. In the fall he would go back to teaching at the Sorbonne. "Sometimes I cannot believe the respectable person I have become," he told me, not finding that entirely funny.

He had brought one of his own early books with him, by accident. "I reached for another book and came back with this old primer." Well, it was not exactly a primer; it was a thick, obviously very ambitious book. Seeing its size, I thought of those heavy volumes in his room in the Place d'Italie; when he reached out, his hand must have simply settled on a familiar size. His book was a survey of Socialist thought, from Marx up to the present—it was published in 1965. Plus a long final chapter on the possible future of Socialism. "It is a young man's book. I was much more idealist in those days," Jean-Paul told me, handing it over; I did not remind him that it was only ten years back, when he had been about the age that I was now.

I have found that the most brilliant theoretical exposition is often not the most difficult to understand, and so it was with Jean-Paul. Even when he dealt with what were to me new concepts, economic theories, possible Socialist solutions, he was dazzlingly clear—even in French. I found it all deeply stirring, too: visions of justice, equal chances, an end to starvation and war.

As I read on, at moments I was of course visited by a

suspicion that it was rather Jean-Paul himself to whom I thrilled, the proximity of his sad clear blue eyes, his tall and very lean, now suntanned body. But it seemed to me, really, that both were possible: I could be in love with Jean-Paul and also with ideas of social justice; surely there are much less plausible combinations of affection.

However, it was love that we talked about as we basked, half-naked in the August sun, in the privacy of our porch. We exclaimed at the marvelous smell of each other's sun-warmed skin; sometimes we would begin to kiss and caress each other, and then we would hurry inside and upstairs to our bed.

One way or another, borrowed houses always yield up their owners, at last, in new lights, and Royce's cabin was no exception; its version of Royce was surely one that I had not seen before. The cabin had an appealing, comfortable, lived-in shabbiness, whereas hitherto everything that I had seen of Royce had been so large and expensive—the Stinson Beach house, his cars and his very person. This must have been a house bought early in that ill-fated marriage, for a not-rich young couple with two small growing children.

In one corner of the living room, with its big glass windows facing the lake, there were some bookshelves, and a small, curiously touching library, entirely devoted to studies of the area. Books on wildflowers, birds and local animals, histories of the region, including, inevitably, the luckless Donner Party. Trail maps, contour maps, a map of the lake itself that showed its varying depths. Some old books, some fairly new. All in all, it was the sort of library that could not be calculated—or faked: in my former trade, decorating, I had sometimes been asked to do just that, to manufacture a convincing library. Royce's books were those of a man in love with their subject matter, this area of land, this beautiful

North Tahoe scenery, which of course made him much more sympathetic in my view. I thought too that now we would have a topic of conversation, Royce and I; whenever I saw him, we could talk about how much I had loved this place, and he could tell me more about it.

This was all to happen in some distant future, with Agatha and Royce and me established as old friends.

Sometimes, as Jean-Paul and I talked about Agatha and Royce, Ruth and Caroline, and Tony—of whom I sometimes thought as I looked across the lake to where he probably was —I wondered *why:* why did I happen to become so involved in the violent downfall of that family? What did it mean, my year in California? Jean-Paul laughed at that form of speculation: "It had no meaning at all," he said. "You met them all by accident, because you all were there. It is how history occurs."

Later I thought he was probably right, and sometimes I still think it did not mean anything, especially. But at that romantic moment, that interval of love in the bright mountain air, it seemed to me that all the year had been leading to this one enchanted week with Jean-Paul. I had come to California because Royce was to lend us this house.

Is all determinism ultimately so sentimental? Well, maybe so.

It was sometime during that week that we decided, without much discussion, really—it seemed obvious—that in the fall I would move back to Paris with Jean-Paul. By then I would have finished Agatha's house, and Stacy's. Agatha and Royce could move into their house as Jean-Paul and I moved out. We would cross the country and then the Atlantic, going to the small flat that he now owns, on the Rue de Savoie, in Paris.

All the money that I had earned would come in handy, of course, as well as the money from that crazy chair. In Paris I planned to study furniture design in a serious way. What with the various uncertainties involved in our plan, including Jean-Paul's health, I had, at last, to concentrate on work.

We came to our last afternoon. It was almost hot, and in the faint breeze that rippled the blue blue lake, there was the slightest, yet eerily unmistakable hint of fall, like the dissenting notes of a cello in a sunny quintet, or like falling yellow leaves. Everywhere you looked the scene said summer, all the blue green gold day, and although you desperately wanted to believe that it was summer, and that the summer would last forever, still you knew—you couldn't not know, that autumn was fairly close at hand. I would, at that time, have given anything in the world for time to go back just one week, to let us start our week up there over again. But soon it would be September, then October; and often in November the snows begin around there, I had read in one of Royce's books on local weather.

I wondered if we would be warm enough in Jean-Paul's flat, but I couldn't exactly ask him.

In fact there were quite a few dangers in our plan, and I made an effort to force myself to think of them, to face them. One of course was Jean-Paul's emphysema. I had asked Agatha about it before we left San Francisco, but what she said was rather vague: it is not always a "life-threatening" disease; that depends on how badly you have it. Serious, "advanced" cases do kill people off, eventually, and it is not a good way to go. Jean-Paul at first had said that his case was mild, "a touch." And I had not asked again. But what about all that coughing?

Other perils were implicit in the huge romantic risk we took: suppose, in a long-run day-to-day way, we just didn't get along too well? For one thing, our verbal rapport was considerably less than perfect, his excellent English and my fair French notwithstanding. Sometimes it was clear that we were missing each other's drift. However, as I have said, the only person with whom I have ever felt a perfect understanding along those lines was Agatha—and maybe Jacob. I think communication with Jean-Paul will probably improve. Well, I hope so.

Another worry, although minor and silly-sounding, maybe, is that except for physical love, Jean-Paul is not a deeply sensual person. To matters of food and drink he is indifferent, although very polite when I have gone to a lot of trouble with a mustard sauce for salmon, for example. I drink more wine than he does, and food and wine are deeply important to me. He is more like Agatha, really, in that regard, maybe having to do with their both having essentially saintly characters. Anyway, I don't see that as an occasion for trouble. You could have that sort of difference with anyone, unless you find a twin, and that probably wouldn't work out too well either.

Jean-Paul had with him, at Tahoe, a small street map of Paris. I love maps, and I pored over that one, saying aloud to myself the magic names of those streets in the area in which we were going to live: the Boulevard Saint-Germain, and the smaller streets off and around it—the Rue de Seine, Rue Bonaparte, Rue Jacob, Rue du Bac.

And so it was with both exhilaration and apprehension that I thought of our life in Paris.

In any case, that's our plan.

A NOTE ON THE TYPE

This book was set on the Linotype in Janson, a recutting made directly from type cast from matrices long thought to have been made by the Dutchman Anton Janson, who was a practicing type founder in Leipzig during the years 1668–87. However, it has been conclusively demonstrated that these types are actually the work of Nicholas Kis (1650–1702), a Hungarian, who most probably learned his trade from the master Dutch type founder Dirk Voskens. The type is an excellent example of the influential and sturdy Dutch types that prevailed in England up to the time William Caslon developed his own incomparable designs from them.

The book was composed by Fuller Typesetting of Lancaster, Pennsylvania, and printed and bound by The Haddon Craftsmen, Inc., Scranton, Pennsylvania.